CW01096115

The Troublesome
Adventures of

Robert the
Robot

Jack

Enjoy my book!

Mike
Simpson

The Troublesome Adventures of

Robert the Robot

Mike Simpson

Copyright © Mike Simpson 2005

First published June 2005

Published by
Recognition Publishing
Yew Tree House, PO Box 243
KT8 0YE

All rights reserved. No part of this work may be reproduced
or stored in an information retrieval system (other than short
extracts for purposes of review) without the express permission of
the Publishers in writing, nor be otherwise circulated in any form
of binding or cover other than that in which it is
published and without similar condition being imposed
on the subsequent purchaser.

Mike Simpson has asserted his right under the
Copyright, Design and Patents Act 1988 to be identified as author
of this work.

A catalogue record for this title is available from the
British Library

ISBN 0 9537373 2 2

Design and typesetting by Stuart Nichols,
Web Graphics Limited, 5 Lyon Road, Walton on Thames, Surrey
KT12 3PU

Printed and bound by St. Edmundsbury Press,
Blenheim Industrial Park, Newmarket Road,
Bury St. Edmunds, Suffolk, IP33 3TU

Leslie Ann, John and Jack.
Fond memories.
Thanks for the inspiration.

Chapter One

The comic robot strode down the school corridor. Some sort of scrap metal machine with the movements of a soldier marching with a high-kicking step. In his arms he carried Michael's headmaster high in the air, his legs wriggling and his body squirming. Mr. Squinch yelled to be put down, demanding that the tin man let him go. But the grip was firm and the intention definite.

Children crowded every doorway leading off the corridor, straining to see what was happening. Shocked by the appearance of the robot, yet eager to watch the fate of their headmaster, who was now being twirled around like a windmill. It was the most exciting thing that had ever happened at school. Everyone was scrabbling around; the atmosphere electric. Only Michael Dobbins was concerned. Only he was holding his breath. Hoping upon hope that his robot, Robert, wasn't going to do something serious. Now he wished he hadn't made Robert. Hadn't built this robot out of odds and ends, a jumble of erratic junk. It was a dreadful mistake. What a foolish thing to have done.

It had all begun so differently.

1

Michael Dobbins was a lonely child. He had a loving, but often absent family. Hard working mum and dad and a miserable grandmother who had trained as a spy, or so Michael thought. But only two really good friends; schoolmates. And they didn't last. First Peter left the school because his father had taken a job near Manchester and the whole family had to move there. Then the other friend, Charlie, changed school and went to one five miles away, so what with homework and travel Michael never saw him.

Michael was left on his own. And on his own he had to suffer constant bullying from the school goon, Billy Carter. Every playtime he would hide in a dark corner of the playground, trying to make himself invisible.

'Look! There's that idiot without any friends.' Billy Carter shouted out and prodded his finger towards the bowed figure of Michael, hiding behind a girls' game of hopscotch. The gang that Billy led made their way over to Michael. Fear on his face. His knees trembling.

'Oi, no friends! You hiding from us?' Billy taunted.

'No,' Michael replied feebly.

'Got no friends have you, weed?' Billy continued. The rest of his gang laughed. They were having super fun. Nothing like picking on someone. It meant you weren't being targeted.

'You boys get into class.' Mr. Squinch was standing over the group. 'Bell's gone. Get going, now!'

Michael was saved this time. Carter would be back. He wasn't safe forever.

On the way home from school that day he hurried down roads that led away from his house. A long and winding route to avoid the attention of Billy Carter and his gang of nutcases.

Once he had arrived home he grabbed a drink and some biscuits and plonked himself down in front of the telly. His Gran was around the house. He could hear her moaning to herself and cursing everyone else. It was always their fault that she shuffled about, was deaf and unhappy. Michael tried to keep out of her way.

There wasn't much on the box. Some tripe about sailing holidays for kids. Michael ate the chocolate off one side of his biscuit and was about to attack the other side when a fresh programme came on. This caught his attention and he left the game with the biscuit. It was about a robot that a man had designed and built himself. It was fascinating. Michael was glued to the screen.

'Wow.' Michael sat back when it had finished. 'What a brilliant idea. I wonder if I could do it.' He spoke thoughtfully to himself. 'A real friend. One that

I could build. A robot friend.

Sliding back came fond memories. His grandfather had once told him about a robot toy that was around when he was young. Some Yankee contraption. It was called Robert. That's what he would do, he'd call his new robot friend Robert.

It was a crazy idea but there was no discouraging this determined boy.

When he arrived back from school the next day the enthusiasm was still as strong. He began searching for stuff. The sort of stuff you used to build robots. He wasn't totally sure what he was looking for, but he'd know when he saw it. Gran gave him some peculiar looks as he hunted round the house, in the garden, scrambling over junk in the shed and the garage and even spying in the spider-infested loft.

No luck so far, he thought, as he sifted through a cardboard box full of old storage jars. 'Not looking good,' he muttered. He sat back on the ground and scratched his head.

After several minutes fighting against a sickening feeling of failure he decided to stride around the garden, kicking some hanging plants to death. It helped. At a pile of ivy his swinging foot connected with something hard. Clang! An old dustbin that had once been used as an incinerator was hidden beneath. Michael dragged it clear of the vegetation and stood it on the grass. In the failing light he didn't see a rusty old dustbin at all.

'His body. Yes, definitely, Robert's body. Perfect.' It was just what he was looking for. A robot's torso.

Gran was in the kitchen and grumbling about a stain on the carpet. He waited until she had wandered off to another room. It was a struggle to heave the bin in through the small aisle between the units. Just as he was opening the door leading to the basement he was confronted by Gran who was returning to the kitchen.

'What you up to?' A brutal voice. 'You're not bringing that bit of junk in here.'

'It's all right, Gran. Dad said so. It's for a project. For school, see.' The lies came flying out.

When his demonic grandmother had gone back into the lounge Michael hurried down the wooden steps into the chaos of the basement. He cleared a space, where he placed the dustbin. He had Robert's body. Now to find the rest of him.

Behind the garden shed he found a bucket without a handle. A metal one with a hole in it. 'Just right for his head,' Michael said. Things were fitting into place now.

'Feet? What can I do for feet?' Michael puzzled, as he stacked the bucket in the basement next to the dustbin. A wander round the bedrooms gave him the answer. In his Gran's room, which smelt of talcum powder and lavender, he found just the things. Two green biscuit tins, one empty and the other half full. They were long square tins, just like Frankenstein's monster boots. He grabbed the empty tin and started to leave the room. 'Should I?' Michael stopped in his tracks. 'She wouldn't know, would she?' He scuttled back and pulled open the other tin. Crunch! Crunch! One after another he crammed the remaining biscuits into his mouth. So full he couldn't speak. Crumbs everywhere. 'She'll think she's eaten them all. I hope!' he spluttered as he fled from the room with a tin under each arm.

The legs were causing a problem, but nothing was impossible now. He was getting excited by all his success. Secretly he still worried about his Gran finding out about the biscuits. She might be a diabolical foreign spy, but she wasn't completely stupid.

In the garage he found what he was looking for. Paint tins. Empty ones in different sizes. He decided the large emulsion tins stuck together would make the legs. He reckoned about four for each leg. And the smaller tins that once held lacquer would be fine for the arms.

By the time he had wrestled this lot down stairs there was a mountain of his junk sitting on the basement floor. Good job his Dad didn't go down there, and his Mum being scared of spiders she wouldn't dare climb down through the cobwebs to the basement. Gran of course had bad legs and descending steep stairs was off the agenda.

Finally he discovered what he would use for Robert's fingers. In a bottom drawer of his Dad's desk he found a collection of old pens, and in another drawer two empty cigar tubes; aluminium ones with screw ends. Not exactly flexible digits, but there was nothing better. Time was short and Michael wanted to start building his friend as soon as possible.

He was up early on Saturday morning and caught the bus to the high street. Michael knew the man who owned the television shop there, and his dad's old school chum ran the computer store next door.

'Out the back. Take what you want, lad.' Michael was directed by Mr. Smart to a pile of dead TVs, a box of battered parts and dismantled CCTV equipment. He scooped as much as he could carry. Some of it's bound to be useful, he thought.

Next door he had even greater success. 'Haven't got time to use this lot myself, you're welcome to anything that suits. Good luck.' The storeowner handed over some fascinating panels of switches and memory boards, chips and a range of electronic bits and pieces.

Michael struggled home with the two containers

and almost fell through the door to the basement as he quickly hid all this treasure from his nosy Gran, who was hanging about near the dining room door mumbling to herself.

Friday evening. Fumbling construction and a few errors of judgement. He had managed to screw the bucket head on to Robert's body and one leg was nearly complete. Not bad for a boy who had made a real hash of reassembling his mother's vacuum cleaner, when he took it apart just to see how it worked. Inquisitive yes, practical no. Instead of sucking it blew. It had taken him all day to clear up the mess. Even Pepper, the cat, had to suffer the indignity of being bathed - twice. A dangerous operation. Pepper had sharp claws, and a great skill at embedding them into the arms of those who were forcing her into water. Michael's parents were not amused. But that was a long time ago.

By the following Wednesday Michael had put together his robot. Legs attached and arms as well. The fingers were firmly inserted and the biscuit-tin feet secured in place. Not exactly a pretty sight, especially as all the paint tins were splattered with different colours. More like a clown than a robot.

After a few phone calls to his Mum's brother, Uncle Dan, Michael was ready to start wiring up Robert. Two salvaged miniature television cameras were used as eyes, an old stereo speaker for the mouth, microphone ears and several metres of interwoven wires to reach the moving parts in his legs and arms. Michael wasn't able to give the robot joints in his arms or legs and so Robert would have very stiff limbs indeed. A blue plastic bottle-top for Robert's nose. A useless addition, but necessary to complete a recognisable face.

Two car batteries that Michael had charged up in the garage were to be used as the power source, and he lowered them into a compartment built into the dustbin body, that was reached through a door he had engineered in his robot's chest.

Finally he was finished. Michael puffed with exhaustion. It was late on a Friday night when he climbed out of the basement and crept towards his bed.

'What's all that banging and things?' His Gran caught hold of him as he closed the door. 'What you doing down there? Up to no good I bet. You wait 'til I tell your mum and dad.'

'School project, Gran. Special assignment. Can't tell you too much. Exam stuff you see.' Michael quickly dodged past, through a mist of solder smoke, and grabbed a drink from the fridge to sip in bed.

'Kids these days.' Gran shuffled off groaning.

Chapter Two

School couldn't go fast enough the next day. Michael just wanted to get back and try Robert out. Turn him on and make friends. Even a heavy session of bullying at playtime by Billy Carter and his gang was quickly forgotten.

Michael jumped the steps from the basement door. Gran was fiddling about upstairs. Hopefully it was safe.

Robert stood where Michael had left him. A giant metal man surrounded by the junk of the basement. Not moving of course. Waiting for life.

Michael took off his school blazer, rolled up his sleeves, opened the hatch door in Robert's chest and switched on.

He waited.

Nothing.

His eyes watched every part of the robot.

Nothing.

Not even the slightest movement.

Michael wanted to cry. All that work and now this. His robot didn't work.

Eventually he tumbled out of the basement and headed for the tea table, where his Gran was dishing up burnt fish fingers. She grunted as he sat down and sniffed. She always sniffed.

'Eat up. Need food to grow. When I was your age we didn't have much to eat you know.' Gran was off on one. 'Always down there in that basement. You'll be as pale as a turnip, you will.'

Clank! Crundle! Brattle! Tinkle!

From the basement came the sounds of someone knocking over a pyramid of pots and pans in their kitchen.

'What the devil?' Gran shook.

Michael ran. Leapt down the steps two at a time to the basement.

Robert was alive! Shuddering like a misbehaving washing machine in the middle of the room. Two fingers had already fallen off and Michael feared Robert would shake himself to pieces. He grabbed at the switch and turned him off.

It was a mixture of pleasure and concern. He was glad Robert was working, but not sure what was happening to him. After a brief visit upstairs to assure Gran that all was well below Michael spent two hours making adjustments. Wires snaking everywhere and plenty of screws tweaked and corrected.

'Now,' Michael whispered as he switched Robert on again. There was a whirring sound. Robert shook slightly but didn't start vibrating like mad, as he did before. 'Yes. He's working.' Michael was delighted.

Michael watched Robert for several minutes, amazed by his creation. 'What first?' he asked himself. He rubbed his chin. 'Of course, I'll get him to speak.'

Michael faced his robot. Eyes fixed on the camera lenses. 'I want you to know your name. Say *your name is Robert*.'

There was a crackling from the robot's speaker mouth. Michael stared at Robert's face, urging him to mumble his name.

Like a voice from someone trapped down a deep metal pipe. Echoing as it emerged. A steel recording. 'Your name is Robert.'

Michael was both pleased and disappointed. His robot had spoken, but he had got it wrong. A minor glitch.

'No,' Michael began again, 'your name is Robert.'

'Your name is Robert,' came the metallic voice again.

'No, no, your name is Robert. You are Robert. I'm not Robert.' Michael was losing it.

'I am not Robert,' came the response.

Michael was getting annoyed with his robot's misunderstanding. 'Look, let's get this straight. Me, I'm Michael. My name is Michael.'

'My name is Michael,' Robert responded.

'No! Your name is Robert.'

'Your name is Robert,' Robert insisted.

'Fool!' Michael reached for the switch and disconnected the power. 'Have a rest Robert. You're hopeless.'

All day at school he worried. A robot that couldn't say his name. It was awful. He'd spent so much time building his friend and now it wasn't possible to communicate with him. What good was that? Billy Carter sneered and jostled him as usual, but he ignored these events. There were more serious matters to think about.

At home Gran insisted he ate before 'going down in that dungeon again'. Michael was nervous and opened the basement door cautiously. He was afraid of what was going to happen that evening. Robert stood in the middle of the messy basement. Perfectly still as he had been left. Michael switched him on. There was no sound.

'Hello, Robert.' Michael's voice was low and slow.

A crackling sound came from Robert's speaker, as if he was clearing his throat.

Michael began carefully. A new approach. 'My name is Robert. Say that.'

A pause, and then the crackling changed to a high-pitched whine. Robert was straining to get it right. Even a robot can recognize when he has let someone down.

'Your name is Robert.' Slow and canned.

Michael wanted to weep, but he was determined to continue. 'You are Robert. Just say Robert, Robert, Robert.'

It worked. 'R..o..b..e..r..t.' Slow and deliberate Robert said his name. 'Robert.' Again. This time with more confidence. And again. 'Robert.' A hint of pride now. 'Robert, Robert, Robert.' He carried on.

'Okay, that's great.' Michael let him say it several times before he interfered. 'I'm so glad you've got it. Put me out of my misery, say *I am Robert*. Just for me.'

With the same satisfaction Robert spoke. 'I am Robert,' he announced.

There was no turning back. Robert spoke all that evening. Michael taught his new metal friend as much as he could. His memory chips absorbed it all. And from this base Robert conjured up his own phrases. His personal version of the English language. *Robot Speak* Michael would later call it.

'Goodnight Robert,' Michael whispered as he switched the power off. Wow, was he tired, but what a great time it had been.

Michael couldn't wait. It was all happening. Nothing at school seemed important. All he wanted to do was get back to his friend and spend time teaching him to be a great robot and a good pal.

'Walking, Robert. That's what we are going to do now,' Michael announced as he turned Robert on and sat in front of his expressionless bucket face. 'First we lift the right leg and then the left and we walk. Look.' Michael stood up and strode across a clear patch of the basement. 'Just like this.'

'Yes, Master, walking. That looks very good.' Robert's tinny reply.

'Ready?' asked Michael.

'Ready,' came the metal voice.

Robert lifted his right leg high in the air. No knee joint, so it rose like a straight piece of steel, even though it was a row of paint tins. And then the left leg. Straight up.

Crrraaassshhh!

'Oh, no Robert, you have to put the first leg down before you lift the other, you dolt!' Michael was annoyed at Robert's stupidity.

Michael pulled him up from the floor. Boy, was he heavy. Michael had no idea his creation could weigh so much. There was repair work to be done. A foot was loose, another finger had detached and one of the camera eyes wasn't working. He switched Robert off. It took well over an hour to finish.

'Now listen carefully,' Michael began, as soon as Robert was operating again.

'Yes, Master,' Robert courteously replied.

'Lower one leg before you use the other. Is that clear?'

'Exactly,' Robert agreed, in a voice that sounded like it came from the bottom of an old steel drum.

'Let's try it then,' Michael urged.

Robert lifted his right leg and placed it back down.

'Excellent,' Michael encouraged.

Robert raised his left leg and placed it down. Then the right again. Then the left. Right, left, right, left, right, left. On the spot though. He didn't move. Left, right, left, right. A metal goon going nowhere.

'You have to push forward,' Michael blurted, 'it's no good just stomping up and down on the spot.'

'Of course, Master.' Robert lunged forward. His mechanical legs thrusting him at speed across the basement.

THUD!

Robert smashed into a pile of cardboard boxes that spilled old clothes and a tea-set over the fallen robot.

'Waa!' Michael roared with laughter. 'Good one Robert.'

'Good one? Does that mean Robert did it well?' If he could have smiled he would have been displaying a broad grin on his bucket face.

'Robert did better. Robert made me laugh. It was really funny,' Michael chuckled.

'I am glad I pleased you.' Robert's voice grated through the speaker mouth as Michael helped him upright.

'We just need to perfect the walking,' Michael explained as he set Robert in the ready position. 'Let's start again. Left, right. Just as before.'

Robert took some time to get it right. He walked in circles for long periods, walked backwards and crashed into walls, hopped on one metal leg when the other dragged behind and all manner of odd actions.

Michael laughed, cried and pulled at his hair in frustration.

'Time for bed.' His mother's voice announced from the basement door.

Michael quickly grabbed the door flap at Robert's chest and cut the power.

'Sorry Mum, didn't realise the time.' Michael scuttled past her and shut the door. He didn't want prying eyes. Didn't want his mother to see Robert, his mad, metal friend.

'Don't you do too much. This project seems to be taking up all your time. Hope the rest of your school-work isn't suffering. Gran keeps on moaning about the noise. Try and keep it down a bit.'

'Sure Mum.' Michael ducked under her outstretched arm and made his way to bed. He was really tired.

Friday after school proved a turning point. Robert was getting it right and walking well. Stiff of course but proudly. More like marching. A metal warrior. Back and forth. Up and down. Relishing his next journey.

However, teatime wasn't such a success. On a Friday it was formal, well about as formal as it got in Michael's house. Round the table in the kitchen. Dad home early from work, mother running round dishing up and Gran complaining that she didn't eat fish.

'You should see Jenny's basement next door,' his mother began. Talking half to herself and half to a husband more interested in tucking in to his meal. 'Got it all set up for the kids and themselves. Pool table and a small TV, storage for their boating stuff and carpeted. Ideal for when someone wants to get on quietly with something. Like watching the football without a vacuum cleaner running round their feet. Jenny says that she might use it for guests as well. Get a sofa bed.' She banged some saucepans just to emphasise her point.

'Yeah, well you don't have to keep up with the neighbours do you?' Michael's dad argued.

'Not that at all. Have you seen our basement? No, you haven't. Not been down there lately have you?

It's a right mess. I'm ashamed to show it to anyone. Only the boy who goes down to do his project. So Gran says.' Mum was agitated.

'Show it? Who wants to see it? Storage, that's what it's used for. You don't show people storage areas. Like to see my junk room? Want to see my old school photos and the kids old toys do you? Be sensible, Doris.' Sarcasm from Mr. Dobbins.

'A disgrace! And you are going to leave it like that aren't you?' Mum screamed. A full-blown row was imminent.

'Now, now.' Bill Dobbins needed to defuse the argument. 'I'll have a look at it tomorrow. Pop down there and sort things out.' A submissive tone.

'Huh.' Doris was simmering still as she strode out of the kitchen.

Tomorrow! thought Michael. 'Oh, hell,' he muttered under his breath. If his dad went down there in the morning he'd see Robert, realise what he'd been doing. Michael would be for it, big time.

Chapter Three

The very earliest he had ever got up. Michael slipped out of bed at five o'clock. He didn't appreciate how dark it was at that time, or how chilly. No time for breakfast. Immediately down to the basement. Robert was there. A statue sticking out from the piles of jumble.

'We have to be quick. I don't know what we are going to do with you yet. Dad's going to clear this place. Maybe we can come back when he's fed up with it. Mum was nagging him last night.' Michael jabbered.

Robert listened, knowing only that Michael was flustered.

'Robert is ready. What ever you say, Master.' A robot's clattering tongue.

'Up the stairs. We need to get you up the stairs and to a new hiding place.' Michael hailed him towards the first step. 'I'll push from behind and you concentrate on climbing to the top.'

It was a difficult job. Robert's legs could not bend and he was extremely heavy. Michael took the weight and tried to lift him at the base of his dustbin body.

'Goodness, you are a heavyweight.'

'Sorry, Master,' Robert replied as he struggled to get a hold on the smooth steps with his biscuit tin feet.

On the last step Michael was about to give up. Absolutely shattered. Robert was quite enjoying the experience, and looking forward to his escape from the basement. From above, the sound of a clicking door. Movement from his parents' bedroom. Michael gave one last almighty shove and Robert went flying through the basement door and sprawling across the hall floor.

'What's that?' Gran was already in the kitchen.

'Just dropped a bucket,' Michael responded.

He opened the front door and eased Robert to his feet. With another helping push he encouraged Robert out of the door and up the garden path. 'Left, right, left, right.'

Just in time. His dad trundled down the stairs as Michael was shutting the front door.

'Made it,' gasped Michael. 'Stop there.' He halted Robert at the end of the path. 'Wait a second, I'm whacked.'

'More than a second I think, Master. I will wait thirty. You are tired. I can sense that.' Robert's loudspeaker mouth explained.

'Wow! He can sense things. It's certainly looking up for the robot builder.' Michael felt a little proud.

'Oi! Nofriends. Who's this jerk in the metal suit?' Billy Carter came swaggering past, tapping Robert's metal head. 'Off to a fancy dress party is 'e?' Billy cackled with laughter. 'And what you going as, a stupid idiot with no friends, eh?' More hysterical laughter.

Robert's arm flashed through the air, his long, spiky fingers clanking. With a swiping movement he had him dangling by his shirt collar. The robot held Billy Carter high in the air. No more than a swinging bag of potatoes.

'Put me down! Oi, let go of me.' Billy wasn't laughing now. Oh no, Billy was no longer the brave kid pushing others around. 'Michael, tell him to let go of me. Tell your friend to drop me.'

'Ha, ha, ha.' Now it was Michael laughing. 'How's that feel Billy?'

Robert carried the blubbering boy along the road, swinging in the air. Michael scampered behind, trying to keep up with his striding robot.

'You'll have to put him down soon,' Michael told Robert.

'Robert will put him down, Master.' Robert had stopped, Billy swaying in the air, and was waiting for the panting boy to stand beside him.

Billy Carter shivered with fright. 'Please let me go. Please!' What a snivelling coward he was now.

'I...won't...be nasty...anymore.'

'Robert will put him down. Robert will let him go.' There was a determination in that metal voice.

Robert lifted Billy a little higher. Swung him over the most polluted ditch you'd ever seen. A swamp of green stagnant water that even a frog would hop over and avoid.

'Let go!' Billy Carter's last words before the drop.

Robert's grip loosened and he obeyed. The boy's body slipped from his grasp.

SLURP!

Billy Carter slid into the slimy mud with ease. Hardly a sound above that initial swallowing up by the foul mud. Down he went until only his head was visible, protruding from the stinking goo. Tears in his eyes and a mouth spitting brown liquid. A mixture of pleading words and vile water.

'Help!' Billy Carter gurgled. 'I'm goin't' die.'

Michael was finding the whole scene really funny, yet he worried that his robot had gone too far. 'Is he all right there?' Michael asked. A stupid question really; how would a robot know.

'Billy Carter is fine.' Even Robert's echoing voice sounded as if he was holding back a loud chuckle.

'I'm sinking,' Billy Carter spluttered.

'No, you're stinking,' Michael added, grinning like mad.

Billy Carter was sinking. His mouth slowly slid beneath the muck, and bubbles formed at his nose. Michael loved the silence. No more names. No more violence. No more fear.

'Better get him out now,' Michael instructed Robert.

'Yes, Master.' Robert pushed his pen fingers into the mud and found Billy's collar. With one upward movement he pulled the boy clear. With a rich BURP! his body came clear. For a moment a hole remained where he had been stuck in the ditch. This gradually disappeared as the gunge filled in the hollow Billy Carter had left.

In the air he dripped foul fluid. He murmured something that Michael couldn't make out. A fallen bully. He wouldn't threaten or hurt anyone for a long time. A shaking miserable wretch. Robert lowered him onto the grassy bank. Billy cried for some time. Michael enjoyed the sight immensely. Eventually Billy crawled towards home. Like a slug returning to some slimy hideaway.

'I think we overdid that slightly,' Michael informed Robert. 'But then again it was fun, wasn't it?'

'Most certainly,' Robert acknowledged, stretching out his buckled fingers.

Michael looked around. There was still time to kill. His dad would be throwing things around in the basement and it wasn't safe to return home. In the distance he noticed the distinct blue lights decorating the top of a white patrol car. The Police!

'Quick Robert, we have to go.' Michael pulled at Robert's arm and dragged him towards the road. 'We have to head over there.' He pointed at the park and the library beyond.

At the roadside many of the people in the cars were slowing down to look at the weird metal person and the small boy.

'Robots! My friends.' Robert blurted, and started to walk in the road. Cars screeched to a halt. Robert stroked their bonnets. 'Just like Robert,' he said as he spoke to the front grills of the cars. 'They are robots on wheels. Just like Robert. Robert wants wheels.'

'No, Robert, they're cars not robots, you iron-headed, bucket brain.' Michael pulled him again, but Robert was reluctant to leave his new friends.

When they reached the other side of the road Robert was still looking back to see the glorious colours of the wheeled robots.

The police car had stopped in the traffic. An officer climbed out to discover what was wrong. There wasn't an accident so why were the cars stopped, he puzzled.

Michael almost kicked Robert to get him out of sight. 'In here.' Michael dragged him into the entrance to the library. Robert clanked awkwardly. Loud and disturbing metal noises to announce his arrival.

Inside all was quiet. Hopefully empty.

No such luck. A woman wielding a rubber stamp and with spectacles on a string spoke without looking up. 'Yes?' she asked.

Before Michael could answer Robert spoke. 'Books. These are books.' A crazy voice echoing his hard disk knowledge bank.

'Of course they're books, this is a library you silly...' The librarian looked up '...tin man?' She stood up sharply and tried to scream, but nothing came out. Her body shook and legs were a tremor. 'Are...are you a member?' she struggled to ask.

'I am,' said Michael, 'and this is my cousin from America,' he desperately tried to explain. 'He's an astronaut. This is his uniform. To travel into space.' It was a pathetic tale. 'Sorry if he scared you, miss.'

The woman calmed down at the sound of a reasonable explanation. 'He clanks when he walks. Can't he take it off?'

'Oh, no. See he has been exposed to radiation whilst on a mission, and it would be a danger to us all if he did.' Michael was creative. Surprised himself.

'May I politely ask you to leave then,' the woman said, apologetically. 'Can't have any fall-out in the municipal library, can we? Council are pretty fussy about these things, you know.'

Michael looked out of the window. The police car was pulling away and the traffic was flowing again.

'Right. I'll take my cousin home then.'

'Thank you dear.' A friendly voice now. Relief that this strange person was leaving her beloved library. 'Do come again, er? American person.' Nervy words to Robert.

'I will,' Robert sharply replied. 'I like books. I think.'

Getting home was no easy task. Robert wasn't quite sure about several metal objects he encountered. He was certain that there were other robots in this world, and he took every opportunity to seek out a friendly face, or dial, or electrical circuit. At the municipal car park he struck up a one-sided conversation with a *Pay-and-Display* ticket machine. Looking straight at the screen displaying money inserted and parking status, Robert started to enquire about the machine's health, wealth and happiness. In particular he wanted to ask about his legs, well leg. The contraption stood on a single steel pole, and Robert was determined to discover what had happened.

'An accident was it?' he quizzed, a little embarrassed to have to ask. 'Painful losing it? Slows you down I suppose. Difficult to move very fast when you're hopping along on just the one?'

The machine's lack of progress answered Robert's question for him. Robert raised a hand to comfort his new friend. 'Have to just stand there, do you? Not much fun I expect.' Robert was determined to help out. To support a fellow robot. 'Let me provide assistance.' Robert wrapped his paint-tin arms around the ticket machine and heaved the steel pole out of the ground, taking a huge chunk of concrete with it. 'There!' And with slow steps he carried his *friend* along the road to catch up with Michael.

'What on earth have you got there?' Michael couldn't recognise the Pay and Display unit from that angle. 'Let me see.'

'A new friend. Robert has a new friend. Only one leg. Poor friend.' Robert lowered the metal box to the floor. 'See, poor friend.'

'Dolt! You idiot. That's a parking ticket machine. You'll have the council or the police after us. Leave it. Let's go.' Michael was more than concerned.

'Machine? No, this is a friend. Robot like Robert.'

'No it's not!' Michael was frantic. 'It's a thing you put money in and a ticket comes out. It's not a robot, you daft fool. I would show you, but of course you have yanked it out of the ground and disconnected the electricity.' Michael pulled at Robert's arm. 'Come on. Leave it there. We have to go, and fast.'

Robert placed it on the pavement. Like laying down a body. A sad robot. 'Goodbye, friend,' he whispered as he crept away.

On arriving at his house Michael stopped at the gate and placed Robert behind a car. He had to check that the coast was clear. Robert didn't mind. He chatted to the vehicle as if it was another long-lost friend.

'Come on, he's gone. Probably fed up with all the work.' Michael had to haul Robert away from the car. Robert waved as he left. 'Quiet robot. Didn't say a word. Do you think he is ill?' Robert was concerned.

'It's a motorcar you dense metal-head! I've told you. An automobile. Look that up in your encyclopaedia when you get a chance. You'll be heartbroken. It's no robot.' Michael informed him cruelly.

'What a day,' Michael chirped to himself over dinner. His mum congratulated her husband on the fine effort begun in the basement, and sarcastically inferred that when he had finished, it would be a job well done. His dad and Gran growled a lot. Robert was idle in the basement. A tidier home that evening.

Michael tinkered with Robert when he could during Sunday, but didn't introduce him to anything new. Too much activity and excitement the previous day.

Chapter Four

Michael was dreading school on Monday. Billy Carter would be out for revenge. A low profile was needed.

What he hadn't reckoned on was the frantic adventures that would follow him that fateful day. When you tinker with robots you should always make certain you've switched them off when you finish. Never forget that final check. Michael had forgotten. And when Robert heard his master leave the house for school that morning he cranked and blustered up the basement stairs, and burst out of the front door to track his master down. Like a faithful dog he was in pursuit.

Robert was some time behind Michael and it was well into morning school before the robot arrived. Running pupils and high-pitched screams heralded the arrival of the *monster*. That's what girls were shouting when they saw Robert clomping down the corridor in search of his master. At every door he peered through the window to look for him. And when he was spotted the whole class stood and yelled in fear, even boys who called themselves brave. No one had ever seen such a frightening figure before. There were the most laughable scenes in the cooking class, as flour and fruit were thrown at the bucket head that peeked through the door, and even a tomato or two was chucked.

It didn't take long for the headmaster, Mr. Squinch, to hear of the intruder who was scaring everyone in the building. 'Take me to this thing,' he demanded of his deputy.

'Yes, Mr. Squinch,' the timid man agreed.

When the headmaster found Robert he was peering directly at Billy Carter through a half open door. Billy was under a desk shaking with fear. 'That's 'im that done it to me,' he was blubbering. His gang had disowned him. He was no longer the great leader. *A right girl* that's what he was now, someone had muttered.

'You, you there!' Squinch called. 'What on earth are you doing in my school?'

Michael came running from his history lesson, just in time to see his headmaster confront Robert. 'He's with me, sir. One of my Dad's friends. Dressing up. A joker. He's a right jester, sir. Sorry about this. I'll see him out of school, okay?'

'Stay where you are Michael Dobbins.' Squinch held out his hand. 'I demand an explanation.'

'I'll deal with it, sir. Don't worry.' Michael pulled at Robert's paint-tin arm.

'No, boy! Leave him alone. He's a trespasser and I

will deal with him, all right.' Squinch grabbed Michael's collar, lifting him off the floor and dragging him back.

Robert reacted quickly, as any friend or minder would. He grasped the headmaster's arm and swung him round so rapidly that Squinch lost the grip he had on Michael.

'Leave him alone.' Robert's mechanical booming voice echoed down the corridor. Pupils who were leaning out of open doors dashed back into the classroom and hid again.

Robert held Squinch high in the air, much like he held Billy Carter. His legs wriggled and his face went scarlet.

'Put me down immediately!' Squinch shrieked and waved his free hand about.

Faces appeared at doors again. There was a ripple of giggling.

'You must not hurt small boys!' Robert blasted through his speaker mouth into Squinch's ear.

'I'll report you to the education authorities and the police my good fellow. This is a monstrous act. This is my school and I demand you do as I say.' Squinch blurted on from his position near the ceiling.

Robert decided on action. Slowly, with careful strides he took the cackling headmaster along the corridor. Handfuls of kids crept out of their classrooms and followed. Just like the Pied Piper of Hamlyn.

Michael kept a few feet back, terrified. What was Robert going to do next?

He didn't have long to wait. Robert halted outside the boys' toilets. For a moment he paused, allowing the revolving headmaster to slowly settle in position. Two boys who had been inside the bogs slid out of the door. Robert then proceeded to push the dangling headmaster through the swinging door into the lavatory. In the corner a cistern could be heard filling up. It was a stinking place; a foul stench of stale urine and other revolting odours wafted around.

'Let me go.' Squinch's demands were feeble now.

Robert pushed him into the nearest cubicle. With his free ballpoint fingers he pulled up the seat. Slowly he lowered Squinch, twisting him over as he descended. His head inches from the water at bottom of the pan.

'No, not in here.' A weak voice squeaked. 'Put me down.'

And Robert did. **Down the toilet!**

Robert shoved Squinch's head deep into the toilet pan. Ramming it so hard it stuck.

Squinch tried to speak, but only a bubbling, splattering sound came from the bottom of the bowl.

Robert grabbed the chain and pulled it hard. A

violent rush of flushing water covered the headmaster's bald head and filled up nearly to his ears. Michael was scared Squinch would drown. Luckily the water drained past Squinch's neck. His legs stood out of the pan like octopus arms, thrashing about. Squinch struggled to pull his head free. Robert flushed again.

'Better get him out now,' Michael suggested, suppressing his laughter.

'If you say so, Master.' Robert caught hold of the swaying legs and gave the headmaster's heavy cord trousers a yank. Off they came. Leaving a very flabby bottom now only covered by a pair of awful purple jockey underpants.

Pupils who had spilled through doorway of the boys toilet laughed hysterically at the sight of their headmaster's crinkly bum wobbling in the air.

'Get him out, for God's sake, Robert!' Michael was more than a little tense now. He frantically fed Squinch's trousers back onto his stubby, stubbly legs. Loose, but enough for modesty to be regained.

Robert grabbed the wriggling legs and tugged.

There was a rich **PLOP!** as Squinch's head was unplugged from the toilet pan. Such was the dramatic loss of suction that Robert's action withdrew the headmaster at an alarming pace. Robert held on tightly to Squinch's loosely-fitting trousers. With the force Squinch flew out of them. The headmaster went through the air in his underpants, like a teacher superhero, and SPLAT! into the opposite wall. Just where the boys' urinal was. The blocked one that caretaker, Wallop, hadn't fixed yet, still swimming in a rich yellow liquid. Stinking pee. And topped with foam and floating gum wrappers. Squinch landed against the dripping wall and slid down until he sat in the dammed fluid. His crumpled purple pants soaked up pints of the offensive broth.

A scrum of kids that filled the door roared with laughter. Michael strained not to join them. This was a serious matter. He scooped up Squinch's trousers and left them near to the stinking headmaster who was dazed but conscious. Dripping with stale urine Squinch managed to waddle past the sniggering line of pupils.

Michael was busy ensuring peace was restored. He failed to watch his robot as carefully as he should have.

Robert left the toilet to the applause of the whole school. They had never had such fun. And it hadn't finished. Robert was searching for other ways to help his master. Robert strolled down the corridor. Abruptly stopping at Mrs. Ramsbottom's room, where she taught domestic science. Cooking. Inside, the tables were full of ingredients, left there by students who had hurried out to view the most amusing scenes in the boys' toilet. Robert couldn't resist. He stopped at the first table and dipped his fingers into all the containers. Making Christmas cakes was the lesson in progress and there were all sorts of mixtures and decorations.

Robert smeared himself with as much icing as he could find. It was super looking like a snowman. Onto the gluey coating he sprinkled chocolate buttons, multi-coloured sweets, silver balls made from sugar and many other delicious and fancy candy. And to crown it all he placed a lighted candle right in the middle of the top of his bucket head.

When he stepped out into the corridor he was greeted by a group of children who had been huddled around the door. They yelled with delight as he emerged.

Michael heard the noise and came running. 'Where is he? What's he up to now?' Michael grabbed at the sleeves of students rushing past.

Robert was also searching. He wanted to show off his appearance to his master. In the school hall there was no sign of him. Robert approached the stage where the school plays were performed. No Michael. Robert pulled the large drape curtains apart. They swished back and surrounded the robot. Icing smeared the material and then...flames! The candle on his head had ignited the thick curtains. Flames flashed and sizzled. High to the ceiling, and spread to nearby stage props. The school hall was soon ablaze.

Michael ran in. He knew at once who was responsible. 'Where are you? You stupid rust bucket!'

'Sorry, Master,' Robert croaked from the centre of the stage, engulfed in flames.

'Get out of there. You look like a Christmas cake in an oven. When are you going to do something right?'

'All you lot out of here.' A teacher was organising now. 'Pull those curtains down and fetch some water to put the flames out.'

Instructions aimed at senior children and not Robert, but to be helpful and perhaps pacify his master, Robert headed back to the toilets. With one tug he had the pipes off the wall. Jets of high-pressure water gushed out, and piercing squirts blasted the ceiling. A tidal wave of water surged down the corridor, and hit the school hall like a tsunami. The flames hissed and thick grey smoke replaced the inferno. Charred material, scorched walls, smouldering woodwork and an indoor lake. The school was an absolute disaster. Hadn't Robert done well!

'Come on you!' Michael called out. 'Home, Robert now.' Michael pulled him towards the school exit and down the front steps. 'God knows what trouble I'm going to be in tomorrow.'

Billy Carter was hiding in the bushes as they marched past. A shivering coward, a shadow of his former self. He wouldn't threaten Michael's happiness again.

The police called round at seven that evening. *A vicious assault on the headmaster of Granford Manor School, and wanton destruction of County property. The culprit a man wearing a strange outfit. As if for fancy dress, going as a tin man. Most odd getup indeed. Queer speaking voice and manner. Mr. Squinch was at home resting. An appalling episode.*

'Seems he knew your son and was last seen leaving the school with him,' the constable explained.

Michael's parents knew nothing and were thoroughly bemused by the policeman's visit. Michael was hauled from in front of the television. His knees were shaking.

'Police here, my boy,' his father announced, 'about some lunatic at the school dressed up like a robot. Manhandled old Squinch. Says you were with him. What do you know about this?'

Michael was prepared. 'Oh, him. I just saw him at the school. Didn't know him. Saw what he'd done to the head and the mess he'd made in the school hall. Made sure he left.' Michael was convincing.

'Good boy.' Michael's father was proud. A heroic act

by his boy. 'That clear it up, officer?' he asked, hand firmly laid on his son's shoulder.

'Well,' the policeman was confused, 'I was led to believe different to that.' He studied the notes on his pad. 'You sure you didn't know this man?'

'No.' What an angel Michael looked. Blue eyes and monkey smile.

'Thank you sir, ma'am, son.' The constable touched his cap and left. Still puzzled by the red herring.

As soon as the family had settled in front of the telly for the evening Michael crept down to see Robert.

In amongst the rubble of the basement he looked quite harmless, but the events of the day had proved otherwise. Robert was dangerous. That's how Michael felt.

It took Michael the best part of three hours to dismantle his robot and store him in five cardboard boxes and an assortment of bags. Tears swelled in his eyes as he placed the head in one box by itself. In such a short time he had become very attached to his friend, Robert.

Robert would be stored incognito and well hidden in the attic once everything had settled down, and the house was asleep.

Unknown to Michael there remained sufficient electric charge in Robert's head for him to sense his body being removed and the box-lid closing. If he could have shed tears he would have. But he was crying somewhere deep inside his memory chips and sobbing at his hard disk.

Chapter Five

Dust had settled on the cardboard boxes locked in the attic. Lost items, anonymously sunk in a sea of junk. Robert was only a cloudy memory. Michael had made new friends and didn't need his robot. Selfish in a way, but then again understandable, Robert had caused a lot of trouble for Michael. Kids had been eager to be pals with the robot-maker after the incident at school. He was quite a celebrity. Squinch had left on medical grounds and Billy Carter didn't bully anyone, which made Michael Dobbins the new hero of Granford Manor School.

Two terms after Squinch's dive into the toilet a new boy joined the school, Donald Clipper. A devious boy who had been expelled from three of his previous schools. And whose parents had gone to South Africa to escape their appalling son. Left him at home being looked after by a really weird relation, Uncle Jasper.

It wasn't long before Donald heard the scrumptious stories about the robot that had dunked the headmaster in the boys' bog. He was intrigued by these fascinating tales and sought out Michael Dobbins. He had dreams about a robot that would obey him. His plan was to befriend the boy who had made this mechanical man. His devilish mind was working overtime. Evil plans to get his hands on Robert.

'Name's Clipper, Donald Clipper.' During break he found Michael. 'I'm new. No friends yet.' A smile.

'I know how that feels,' Michael was quick to acknowledge. 'When I first started here it was awful. You can count on me to be a friend.' Michael bounded away with his new group of pals. A reassuring grin.

'Got him.' Donald Clipper rubbed his hands. 'He's mine. What a jerk.' Donald crept back to class happy that he had made contact. His plan was taking shape.

Over the next few days Donald would deliberately run into Michael in school and outside. Talking about all sorts of subjects he considered Michael would be interested in. One Friday lunchtime he mentioned it. Just in passing. Trying to get Michael to open up. 'Did you see those robots on telly last night?' he casually asked.

'No.' Michael tried to deflect the question.

'Great laugh, should have seen it.' Donald wanted to persist with the subject. 'Super machines. Bet they were hard to make.'

'Not that hard.' Michael didn't mean to say it.

'Not hard? What do you mean?' Donald was quickly in.

'Sorry, I wasn't thinking.' Michael tried to escape.

'No, no. What do you know about robot making?' Donald quizzed.

'Well...did it myself once. Long time ago. Don't like to think about it.' Michael weakly admitted.

'Wow! Come on Michael, spill the beans. That's fantastic.' Donald was excited. He'd got Michael telling him now. 'Where's your robot?'

'Gone, I'm afraid.'

'Gone? Where?' Donald's voice went flat.

'He's in boxes and bags. In the loft.' Michael's departing words as he ran off to join a group of children calling him over.

It was enough. Donald Clipper could plan from there. Devilish plans that he would need his wicked Uncle Jasper to help him with.

*

'Gas leak, Mrs. Dobbins,' said the man in the overall at the door.

'Gas leak?' quizzed Gran. 'Ain't heard nothing about a gas leak.'

'All up the street dear. Piping problem. Wrong pipes these ones. For the new supply. It'll only take a short while. Just need to adjust the input valve. All right if I come in?' Uncle Jasper made a convincing gasman.

'Where you going?' Gran asked as Jasper climbed the stairs towards the attic.

'Pipes, ma'am, pipes.' Jasper answered from the landing.

'Gas pipes are down 'ere,' Gran insisted.

Jasper thought quickly. 'Overflow gas. Expansion system.' Any words that sounded okay would do. He was good at deceiving people.

'What?' Gran was confused. 'Ah, get on with it.' Gran shuffled through to the kitchen. 'Too old for all this,' she muttered.

Jasper pushed open the entrance to the loft. Dust fluttered down into his eyes. He faced a pile of discarded and unwanted items. A mountain of rubbish.

'Where is it?' Jasper clambered over piles of coats and spilling boxes.

After forty minutes he hadn't found a robot or anything that looked like one. 'That nephew of mine has got me on a wild goose chase. There's no robot in amongst this junk.'

'You finished up there yet?' Gran stood below the ladder. 'Should be done by now.'

'Nearly done, love. Be down in a second.' Jasper dumped another box across the loft and decided to open just one more. Inside two biscuit tins were attached to some paint tins. 'That's strange.' Jasper thought aloud. He pulled out the tins. Wires seemed to travel through the paint cans and into the green tins. At intervals along the wires were condensers and other computer electronics. 'Yes!' Jasper knew enough about such things to realise this was what he was looking for. It was part of the robot.

'Done are you?' Gran asked as Jasper jumped the last rung of the ladder.

'Yes, thank you ma'am.'

Back at Donald Clipper's house Donald waited for his uncle to arrive.

'Well?' Donald quizzed as soon as his uncle reached the front door.

'Yes! I've found your robot. Well I've found part of him. In boxes in the corner of that idiot's attic. Quite a sophisticated invention he's put together.' Jasper drooled.

'Good. My plan is working.' Donald dribbled with delight.

'Need to get the parts out and then we can put the robot together.' Jasper was looking forward to building Robert.

'Remember, Uncle, this robot is mine. Thanks for your assistance but he's mine, all mine.' Donald was getting possessive.

'I know.' Jasper would play along, although he wished he could get his hands on the robot. He had his own evil plans.

*

'What now?' Gran moaned when she was faced by the same gasman who had annoyed her only days before. 'What do you want now?'

'Just some adjustments, dear,' Jasper told her, as he pushed past and headed for the attic hatch.

'Manners. No manners people these days,' Gran mumbled as she scuffed her way back to the warmth of the kitchen.

It didn't take long for Jasper to locate the boxes he needed. 'Just need the head.' He tossed bags and suitcases aside in his search.

Robert heard the noise. Thought it was his master who had come to rebuild him. To have more fun. It would be so good to have his body back.

'Ah, there you are my beauty.' Jasper had found the old bucket adorned with mini television cameras. 'What a wonderful head.'

The light blinded Robert even though there was only a meagre scrap of energy left in his sensors. He couldn't see the nasty little man who was lifting him out. But he could hear a strange voice. Quite alien to him. Rocked and shaken, swung and lowered. If a robot can be frightened then Robert was frightened.

Jasper bundled the head into a sack. At the entrance to the loft he listened. Waited for the old bag to disappear to the other end of the house and started to unload bags and boxes. He managed to get nearly all of it out to his van before Gran came trundling along the hallway. Uncle Jasper had the last piece of baggage under his arm when he came face to face with the grumbling woman.

'What's that?' Gran was alerted by the gasman carrying a parcel.

Jasper had to think quickly. 'Had to change your expansion bottle. Hydraulic backflow replacement mechanism. Just have to dump this old one.' He pushed past the old lady who almost filled the hall.

'Never 'ad that nonsense when I were a youngster, no.' Gran was flummoxed. Nothing new.

'Got it?' Donald Clipper asked as Uncle Jasper burst through the door. 'Have you got my robot?'

'I have it. All of him. Bit by bit I smuggled that robot out of the boy's attic.' It was quite an achievement and Jasper was looking for praise.

'Let me see, let me see.' Donald pushed past Jasper to get a look at the prize. He pulled open each package or box and examined the parts carefully. 'Doesn't look much.' A self assembly robot isn't too impressive. 'Pretty manky I reckon.' Disappointment in his voice.

'You expect too much, my boy. Perhaps you wish me to take the sordid metal pieces and keep them for myself. You don't seem to have the same feelings for the scheme as before.' Jasper's slit eyes closed even more, and he showed his teeth in a sinister smile.

'No. Just expected something more...more, you know, like you see on telly. Shining and built of bright materials. Not this stuff.' Donald pulled out the body. 'It's junk. Like what they have at the scrapyard. Old boilers, tanks and cars. Rusty bits.'

'Made from the mere offerings from the home, my boy. Your view is too romantic. Too much television. This is the real world. We have a robot. Forget the looks. An ugly robot rather than a filmstar. Don't let it worry you.' Jasper tried to comfort his nephew.

'S'pose you're right. You sure we can put all this together to make him? Seems worse than a jigsaw.' Donald was resigned to having a dumb looking robot. Now his worries centred on the ability to build him.

'Trust me. Uncle Jasper will give you the finest robot in the land.' Jasper fancied himself as a genius with such gadgets.

True to his word, it only took Jasper three days to have the pieces connected and ready for internal fitments.

'Look, Donald.' Jasper stood proudly in front of the freshly constructed Robert. It was a job well done. Okay, he'd made a few mistakes with the paint tins and the head didn't look very secure, but it was definitely Robert. Nose crooked. Jasper had trodden on it but screwed it on, in a fashion, anyway.

'Great!' Donald walked round the robot. More

Robert the Retarded Robot, sagging legs and wonky biscuit tin feet. 'Thanks a lot uncle.' That's about as grateful as he would get. 'And the inside? Electronics and stuff?'

'I'll sort that out. No problem.' Jasper's lips curled and he smiled through Venetian blind eyes. Glinting slits.

It was not as easy as he had imagined, but a lot of cursing and hours of toil and he was ready to display the finished product.

'There are wires everywhere.' Donald marched round in inspection.

'A necessity my dear boy.' Jasper was spitting with anticipation. 'All is in place. We only have to connect up the batteries and we are there. Your skilful uncle has yet again mastered the intricate craft for your enjoyment.'

'What are you on about?' Donald didn't like it when Jasper got smug.

'See here. This is the switch. Just one flick and your robot will spring to life.' Jasper let out a sinister chuckle, reminiscent of a deranged witch.

'Let's get started.' Donald was impatient. Rubbing his hands and letting out small bursts of air from his pouting lips.

With a snapping click Donald created life. His dream was to come true. A robot at his bidding that would obey his evil commands, initiate a dreadful agenda of disgusting deeds.

Donald and Jasper waited. There was nothing.

'What's wrong?' Donald wailed.

'A minute fault. Perhaps a wire. Let me look in here.' Jasper rambled and headed for Robert's control hatch, screwdriver at the ready.

Inside, Robert's head was spinning. Power suddenly reaching his microchips and his hard disk. Time to reassess. After such a long break this mechanism was taking some time to warm up.

'His hand!' Donald shrieked like a little girl. 'It moved, it definitely moved.'

Jasper smiled through his teeth. 'See nephew, I told you I would provide you with your dream.'

Robert began moving all his parts. Testing them out. Creaky joints being eased and electrical circuits buzzing and crackling. His whole body swung round. Even in his previous form the bucket head wouldn't swivel. A coarse, clattering sound, like someone stirring an iron rod into the workings of a huge clock.

'Where...am...I?' A voice from the gravelly bottom of a dumped water tank. Croaking and grating.

'Fantastic! He can speak.' Donald rubbed his hands. Just like Fagin successfully training a boy to pick pockets. 'My own speaking robot.'

'There, my boy. Am I not a genius? Such brilliance.'

Jasper gloated.

Robert faced both of them in turn. Slowly twisting this way and then that. 'Who are you?' Clearer and metallic. 'Where is my master?'

'You see dunderhead, there have been changes.' Donald walked around Robert, rubbing his chin. 'This is a new team. You can forget that loser, Michael. He didn't want you did he? Locked you up in the attic; in bits. No, you're our robot now.'

Robert's hard disk ground away. He was processing the new information.

'Let me introduce the fresh faces.' Donald dribbled and sucked it back with a rich slurp. 'This is my Uncle Jasper, and I am Donald your new master.' He polished his knuckles on his chest. Proud.

'My master is Michael,' Robert sharply retorted.

'No tin man, that's history. He's gone. This is home and I'm pulling the strings.' Donald began to seethe.

'My master is Michael.' Robert's determined voice had increased in volume.

'Jasper, this lump of metal needs reprogramming right away.' Donald turned to his uncle.

'Leave it to me.' Jasper switched Robert off and fetched his toolbox.

'He has to know, Jasper, who is boss. Who is in control.' Donald paced up and down as Jasper fiddled with bits and pieces, poked and prodded, tugged and wrestled.

'He will. I believe I have it fixed. Disposed of the program that the idiot, Michael, had installed. Basic stuff. No real expertise like yours truly.' Jasper beckoned his nephew to restart the Robot.

Robert's circuits hummed. He stood empty-headed and motionless.

'I am your master. My name is Donald.' The conditioning process had begun. 'You are Trevor, my robot. Say these things.'

It was the same metallic voice. But it was different. Hollow and lost. 'Donald is my master. My name is Trevor.'

'Excellent.' Donald was excited. 'Not a bad job, Uncle Jasper.' Praise indeed from the vile boy.

Jasper purred with conceit.

'The test. Now to see if our robot can deliver the goods.' Donald was eager to begin his evil campaign.

Chapter Six

'Trevor, listen very carefully,' Donald began. 'This should be easy for you.' He wandered around the bewildered robot, motionless in the centre of the room. 'I want you to get me *money*. I love money. I really do.' Donald rubbed his hands.

Jasper followed suit.

'We have a mission for you. Go now, Trevor. Go along this road.' Donald pointed out of the window. 'Turn left. When you reach the main road you will see the petrol station on your right. Tell the cashier you want all the money. All of it. Do you understand? Bring it to me. Bring me all that beautiful money.' Donald sucked his teeth.

A slightly confused Robert clunked out the front door and rattled up the road. A steady march. He reached the petrol station with little trouble. The cashier, a young girl name of Chloe, sat studying her nails. Business was slack. Robert opened the door with a brutal kick from his biscuit-tin right foot.

'What on earth!' Chloe exclaimed. Then struck dumb, eyes bulging and mouth fixed open.

'My master wants money.' Robert explained in best tinny English.

Chloe didn't move or speak.

'Money.' Robert held out his paint pot arm, pen finger extended.

Chloe managed to raise a hand and operate the till. The drawer sprang open.

Robert tipped the money out. Coins that he scooped up and built to a pile in his entangled fingers. The notes sat clipped in their compartments. He had no need of paper. Money was metal.

Aluminium cigar tubes and old pens do not fit tightly around a heap of skidding coins. Out of Robert's hands they tumbled as he strode back to Donald Clipper's house. Leaving a trail.

'Here he comes.' Jasper was look-out and spied the returning robot clanking up the road.

'Money!' Donald was ecstatic as he waited in the doorway.

'Here, I have it.' Robert spoke without any pride in this venture. He held out his cupped hands displaying what was left of his spoils. A few measly copper coins.

'What is this?' Donald was fuming. 'You stupid tin can! You have brought me just coins. Where are the notes? Real money.'

'There's a problem, nephew.' Jasper tugged at Donald's shoulder. 'It's all up the road.'

'What is?' Donald was still berating his robot.

'Coins! He's left a trail. Anyone could follow it. We're doomed!'

Donald squeezed past Robert and looked up the path. Every few feet there was a shiny metal disc, a giveaway; leading the treasure hunter to the Clipper house.

'Get them, Trevor. Get them now. Pick up every coin,' Donald demanded.

Robert twisted on the spot, tumbled down the path and proceeded to locate the fallen bounty.

'Put them in this.' Jasper held out a plastic bag. 'And make it quick, they could be onto us already.'

Slowly but surely Robert stooped and collected each coin. Sparks often flying from his metal fingers as he scrapped at the paving slabs.

Almost half way back to the garage, Robert was chasing a reluctant fifty pence piece that was sliding away from his plucking fingers.

'What have we here?' Two shiny black boots were inches from Robert's face, and a gruff voice boomed above him. 'Collecting money in fancy dress are we? On your feet sunshine! Now!'

Robert gave up on the coin and stood upright. Two policemen confronted him. 'I am picking up what I have dropped.' He shook the plastic bag, sagging with loose change.

'You taking the mickey? What's with the idiotic

voice and the iron suit? Get it off and let's see your face.'

'Get what off?' Robert responded in his automaton voice.

'We got a troublesome one 'ere, Harry,' observed the heavier built officer.

'Hand over the bag.' The police constable took hold of the plastic bag still swaying on the arm of the robot.

'My master's money.' Robert snatched it from the policeman's grabbing hand.

'No. This money belongs to the petrol station.' Harry pointed without looking. 'Give it here!'

Robert did not understand. These men wanted to deprive him of the money he had collected for Donald. He remembered how to react. Up went the two policemen. Robert clutched their collars. He knew how to disarm a human. The men swung, blustering and coughing.

'Let us go!' Harry demanded. 'We are officers of the law. You are committing a major crime.'

All Robert knew was that he had to deal with disagreeable men. It was just like Billy Carter and Mr. Squinch. Higher they went. Robert strode toward a towering conifer hedge. Tight foliage, prickly and dry.

'Put us down.' A weak pleading. 'Right now.' Almost a girl's desperate voice.

Robert didn't speak any more. With an arcing, dual bowling movement the two constables were thrust headlong into the scratching hedge. No screams as their heads lodged in the branches. Just low gurgling and whistling whimper. Four highly polished boots protruding from the bush, each quivering slightly.

'I have it.' Robert swung the bag in front of Donald's face.

'Seems clear.' Jasper peered up the road.

'You've covered your trail sure, but I have no *money*,' Donald bleated. He threw the weighty bag to the floor. 'Shrapnel! That's all it is. No good to me.'

'A first run, nephew. Success next time, I'm sure,' Jasper dribbled. 'You'll see. Riches and untold wealth.'

'Yeah.' Donald wasn't convinced. 'Turn him off. Tomorrow we will find out. I have a great plan.' His eyes lit up and he sucked his lips. A wretched boy.

Chapter Seven

Donald waited until dusk the next day before he set his robot in motion. A mere clunk and a low hum from his speaker.

'Trevor.' Donald's brusque voice summoned. 'Trevor, I want you to get something for me. This shouldn't be too difficult. So don't make a pig's ear of this job.' A harsh rebuke. 'Not like the money dropping fiasco.'

'I will get it for you. Whatever you demand...Master.' Robert found it difficult to call Donald that, but something inside fought against a deep-rooted sensation, an pirate microchip some-where. It forced him to utter the word. And he knew he wasn't Trevor. Deep in his hard disk was his real name. He was certain it would eventually unwrap from some distant folder, a maverick connection with a disorientated chip.

'Go to the car showroom. It is along the road.' Donald gestured with his hand. 'A short walk in the other direction.' Donald eyed the crumpled plastic bag still lying on the floor. 'Yes, away from the previous disaster.'

'The Ferrari, Nephew?' Jasper oozed with excite-ment. 'Such style, such power.' He knew he would have to drive his obnoxious little nephew around in the beautiful beast.

'Yes. Go, Trevor, and bring me back a new Ferrari car. There are many to choose from in the showroom. Shiny motors waiting to be stolen.' Saliva flew from Donald's flapping mouth.

Only a few heads turned as Robert scuttled down the road towards the car showroom. Nothing more than intrigue. No fear. He was in character, as the Tin Man from *The Wizard of Oz*, that's all.

Robert stuck his bent plastic nose on the long window that separated him from the row of gleaming automobiles. Every colour was on display. Doors stylishly ajar and bonnets lifted to expose the brutal power of the massive engines. Robert's finger scratched along the window as he slowly inspected every model; his camera eyes picking out the detail. Which one? When he reached the last vehicle he stood baffled. So many to choose from. Robert's head sung. Not enough information to make a selection. He would have to rely on his own judgement. A dangerous ploy.

'Yes!' He was suddenly animated. 'Of course, a wondrous motor car.' Robert pushed closer to the window. This vehicle was not exhibited with the others and he struggled to observe the whole detail. 'Fine colour and design. Unique transportation,' he muttered metallically.

The showroom door was no match for a robot's mechanical strength. Robert wrenched the door off its hinges. An alarm exploded with a heinous screech, announcing the intruder's entrance.

'Yes.' Robert stood at the front of the vehicle he had chosen to take back to Donald Clipper. It was huge and it was orange! It was the tow truck! 'Splendid. A beautiful car.'

Robert climbed into the cab. He ignored the rolled up newspapers and the cigarette ends, the coffee stains and the discarded paper cups. 'Let me see.' Robert talked aloud as if to hear himself think over the panic blasts of the siren still hailing the police. He clutched the steering wheel and waited. Of course this robot had never driven a car before. Enterprisingly he sought help from his hard disk memory. It mentioned a key. Fortunately in his random search for the missing item he happened to tilt the sun visor. A bunch of keys tumbled into his lap. Soon the truck thundered into life, rocking Robert in the seat he had pushed so far back to allow his legs room to reach the pedals. Every metal part of his body chattered and clanked with the throb of the engine. Finding gear was proving difficult, and some ghastly crunching noises echoed the robot's valiant efforts.

A crowd had gathered. Who wouldn't have been hailed by an alarm wailing distress, the heavy purr of a giant diesel engine, the pulverising clunks of a gearbox being destroyed and a weird iron man struggling with the controls of this monster truck. It was pure entertainment. It deserved an audience.

An agile audience at that. They had to be! Robert engaged first gear at the same time as he had full revs of the engine. The tow truck flew through the window of the showroom. Glass splintering and flying in all directions. Almost James Bond. Launched from a standing start and catapulting out onto the road and...straight into the side of the police car just arriving on the scene.

Two police officers carrying the wounds of confrontation. Heavily scratched faces and the look of thunder. It was the two bobbies that Robert had dumped into the undergrowth the previous evening.

Robert's carriage was stalled by the impact. Hardly a mark on the thick orange paintwork. A police car not so fortunate. One side caved in. The stunned policemen crawled out the same offside door; only one of two remaining.

The crowd reassembled; a loose cordon around the collision. Some assisting the stumbling officers of the law. Inside the truck's cab Robert was readjusting himself, somewhat flummoxed by an unexpected take-off and the sudden crash. He ran the program again, and proceeded to start the truck.

'Oi!' P.C. Harry Evans shouted up at the driver of the tow truck that had rammed his squad car. 'Get down here.'

Robert peered from the window. Recognition. An image stored and retrieved. He knew the face, though he'd seen more of his boots.

'It's you!' Harry Evans stepped back a pace. 'Here Pete. It's the blooming tin man who shoved us in the hedge. He's in there. In the ruddy truck that hit us.'

With a splutter the truck roared alive. Robert engaged gear. Forward unfortunately. It pushed the police car across the road. Scraping metal kicking up a firework display of sparks. Once again the spectators scattered. Along with the two police officers.

With a series of jerking manoeuvres Robert managed to direct the truck up the road towards Donald's house. Aware of their duty, but against their better feelings the policemen ran to their wreck of a car and attempted to follow their felon.

'Delay. Nothing but waiting.' Donald paced up and down. 'Where is that metal moron?'

'Patience dear nephew. Trevor is selecting the perfect motor. Making certain he has the very best for you.' Jasper drooled.

Clowns couldn't have conducted a car chase

better. An orange tow truck stuck in first gear whining up the road. All noise and no speed. And behind, a squashed junk of metal, in no way resembling the police car it once was, grating along amidst a shower of sparks. Flickering white light on the sloping roof – the blue cover solidly wedged in the gutter. Slow motion. But enough of a chase to make other drivers wary. Well most!

You couldn't expect Robert to understand every aspect of the Highway Code. Do any of us? But you might consider it a major failing to not realise the importance of a red traffic light. And Robert didn't.

Really it was only a nudge. Maybe a new bonnet, bumper, wing and wheel, and a lot of paint. Nothing too bad. Robert barely realised he had hit it. The driver, a middle-aged man with a ridiculous hat, still sat there staring straight ahead. Had a tin man driving an orange tow truck actually driven through a red light and smashed into his car? And had this been followed by a blazing, disintegrating police car scuttling behind, sounding a muffled version of an emergency vehicle siren? And could it be that inside this load of scrap there were two policemen sporting the faces of a tribal initiation?

There was enough room to get between the parked cars in Donald's road. There definitely was. Not according to the racing robot. Robert managed to collide with at least eight of them. Both sides of the truck were now a wonderful rainbow colour scheme. Long curving lines of deep blues, classic greens, contemporary yellows and an array of other shades. The neighbours were awake and alarmed, and angry. But much to their delight the police were there to catch the culprit. In a fashion. There might have been humour in a different situation. Mr. Plod had never turned up to an incident in such a shabby and ludicrous manner.

The tow truck was stationary. Robert had tangled with a white van and was hauling it down the road, engaging with the next unsuspecting vehicle. Harry had him now. In his sights. At last the *ruddy metal man* was going to get his comeuppance.

Best to test your brakes after a skirmish with a large truck. You never know if a brake line has been damaged. Harry Evans was on him now. He pressed on the pedal. Nothing! He pumped frantically with his stamping foot. Nothing!

Crrrasssh!

'Hell! I can't believe it!' Harry's pressure-cooker head was about to explode.

Robert felt the bump. It did the trick. The white van toppled to the side. A passage through. Straight through to Donald's house. There was no way of knowing the nature of the collision at the back. No way of knowing that the crumpled police car had embedded itself on the towing hook of the truck. No way of knowing he was now towing. Now towing the wrecked police vehicle and the wrecked policemen inside. To a casual observer it might appear that the pursuing vehicle was following its quarry with unquestionable zest. How wrong!

Donald and Jasper heard the commotion. Both were staring from the window. Waiting for their robot to deliver, right outside the front gate, a gorgeous Ferrari sports car. Fiery red, sleek and flashy.

'Is it him?' Donald asked through his teeth.

'Let's hope so,' Jasper slobbered.

'I see something! It's outside. It's...it's...orange. It's...it's...it's a damn truck! The idiot's brought us the stupid tow truck.' Donald's voice slithered to a groan.

'No! Oh no!' Jasper sank to his knees and joined in a moaning duet.

Robert toppled out of the cab, straightened a loose paint tin of his arm and marched up to the house.

He found Donald and Jasper wailing in the front room.

'I have your car, Master. I chose the biggest and the brightest.' Robert tried to smile, but he knew he couldn't. 'Are you pleased?'

Both boy and man were struck dumb. Complete disbelief and disappointment.

'You like your car?' Robert pointed to the huge truck poking above the small conifers in the front garden.

'It's...a...truck,' Jasper finally croaked. 'We said a car...a...Ferrari. That's not...a...Ferrari.' Tears filled his eyes.

'Up the path!' Donald was on his knees peering out of the window. He had found his voice. 'They're coming up the path.' A frantic tone. 'Jasper! I think it's the police.'

And it was. Well sort of. Harry Evans and deputy had squeezed out of the remains of their patrol car. Caps comically askew, torn jackets, stretched ties and absurdly scraped faces. They struggled to remain steady on their legs, and wobbled and tipped on their mission. They had seen the metal prankster head into the house. An arrest was imminent. Harry muttered almost incoherently into his radio. He needed the cavalry. This was a serious case and reinforcements were necessary. The door was open. They found every-one in the front room.

'Right,' Harry puffed. 'Nobody move. You are not obliged to say anything...well you know the rest.' He hadn't got the breath for all that. 'Pete, take the door.'

The scene they faced baffled both officers. There was their desperate criminal standing with a curious looking man and a boy on his knees by the window.

'You.' Harry Evans pointed at Robert. 'Name?'

'My name is Robert.' As metallic as ever.

'Cut the stupid voice, sunshine.' Harry wasn't having anyone poking fun, and especially this crazy dumbnut who'd thrown him and Pete in the hedge.

'I do not know what you mean.' Robert replied. No change in tone or delivery.

'Having a game, are we? We'll see about that. Don't take no monkey business from the likes of you, I'm telling you.'

'You see Inspector he is a...' Jasper attempted to explain.

'You can put a sock in it, pal. I'll see to you in a moment.' Harry wasn't going to let this get out of control.

'What is your bleeding name?' Harry asked through gritted teeth.

Before Robert could answer Jasper reached out and disconnected the power supply.

'What are you doing?' Harry was going to explode soon.

'He won't talk to you in that silly voice now,' Jasper informed him.

'We'll see. I will ask you one more time. What is

your flipping name?'

Robert stood there motionless. Just a chunk of waste metal.

'I'm talking to you.' Harry rapped the dustbin body. 'Crikey! That's hard.' Harry sucked his knuckles.

'I told you,' Jasper insisted, 'he's a robot and he's switched off and he can't answer you.'

'Robot?' Harry screwed up his face. 'You taking the mickey also?'

'Robot?' It was Pete's turn to question.

'Yes. He's a robot.' Donald climbed to his feet. 'He's been threatening us. Burst in here. We were so frightened. Isn't that right, Uncle?' Quick thinking from such a young head. Such a wicked, scheming head.

'Of...of course. Yes that's it,' Jasper bumbled.

'Something fishy here if I'm not mistaken.' Harry lifted his tatty cap and scratched his scalp. 'Robot? Coming in here? Threatening?'

'Didn't seem that way when we arrived.' Pete was playing detective. Resting a finger on his chin and walking in a circle. 'And you seemed to know how to turn this robot off, didn't you.' He poked a finger toward Jasper. 'If he is a robot.' Pete turned and pushed at Robert's torso. He wobbled on the spot and then overbalanced and fell to the floor with clatter of metal. As if someone had thrown every pot from the kitchen, and topped it off with showering the pile of pans with the contents of the cutlery drawer. Bits fell off. Enough paint tins were dislodged for the policemen to see Robert really was a robot.

'Bleeding hell!' Harry rocked on the spot.

'Blow me down!' Pete was equally stunned.

Jasper and Donald held their breath.

'Hello, hello.' From behind the group still studying the fallen robot the sharpened voice of Sergeant Billet. A station sergeant who didn't like being called out this late at night. Away from his tea and biscuits and some restful paperwork. 'What's happening?'

Harry took him aside and briefed the brittle sergeant, leaving out some of the embarrassing parts. It would be too easy to be the laughing stock at the station. But he wasn't safe yet. Oh no.

'So where is the culprit? The petrol station robber, who assaulted two police officers, stole a garage vehicle and caused untold criminal damage whilst attempting to avoid arrest?' Billet enquired.

No one spoke.

'Well?' Sergeant Billet was not amused. 'Simple question PC Evans.'

'You...see Sergeant. It's like this.'

'Stop waffling man. Where is he?' Billet insisted.

'He's here.' Pete weakly pointed. 'That's him.'

The bodies cleared and Sergeant Billet saw Robert for the first time. 'You having me on? I haven't got time for games. Who is he? What is it?'

'A robot.' Donald offered. He was determined to get out of this hole.

'A ruddy robot?' Sergeant Billet pulled a bulldog expression. 'You think I'm some sort of idiot? Come on son, tell the truth here. You trying to cover for someone?'

Pete approached the fallen lump of metal and gave it a hard tap with his handcuffs. The resulting clunk echoed around the front room. 'There you are Sarg.'

'Let me get this clear.' Sergeant Billet thought about the steaming cup of tea he had left back at the station and the safety of his desk. 'We have numerous crimes to solve here. Serious crimes.' The sergeant cringed. 'And our prime suspect is a...a...a blooming robot!'

Sergeant Billet paused, audibly expelling air out of his nose.

'And what do we do, take him down the station and use a can opener on him?' Billet was seething. 'Who's going to interrogate this piece of metal, eh? You, Harry? Are you going to take the ruddy statement whilst offering him a cup of WD40 lubricant? It's a flipping farce. We will be the laughing stock of the Police Federation. All the other local nicks are sure to take the mickey.'

Sergeant Billet began on a different tack. 'And you

two.' He turned to face Donald and Jasper. 'Where do you fit in?'

'Nothing to do with us.' Jasper spoke for both of them.

'Why is he in here then?' Billet quizzed.

'Er...just came in. Off the street. A dangerous machine. As I said, he threatened us.' Donald wasn't convincing.

'Give this place the once over.' Sergeant Billet ordered the two bobbies into action.

It wasn't long before Pete arrived back in the front room with a collection of wires, Jasper's tool kit and other suspicious materials that had Jasper backing away and Donald sniffling.

'What's all this then?' Sergeant Billet managed a smile. 'This is your ruddy robot isn't it? You've been naughty, haven't you? Made your own robot. Been up to tricks, eh?'

Jasper wiped saliva from his chin and nodded pathetically.

'No. I didn't do it. He made the robot. It was him. I told him not to. I did.' Donald stabbed a finger towards his Uncle Jasper. He had resorted to plan B.

Jasper's eyes widened. The spit in his mouth churned. 'Judas! Traitor!' he snarled.

'Seems we're getting somewhere, Harry.' Sergeant Billet rubbed his chubby hands.

'You.' The sergeant prodded Jasper. 'Switch the tin pot on. I'm interested to hear what he has to say. He can talk can't he?'

'He can.' Harry interjected. 'Talks like one of them electronic weighing machines. Like he's speaking from inside an empty bucket.'

Jasper bent down and flicked the switch. A treacherous grin on his face.

Robert stirred. He tried to stand but one biscuit-tin foot was hanging loose and a few pots on his legs were awry. Robert flopped back down.

'Good heavens!' Sergeant Billet was astonished, and a little unsettled. 'Hello.' He felt so stupid. 'Hello, my name is Sergeant Billet. Do you have a name?'

'I do not know you,' Robert grated.

'Has be got a name?' Sergeant turned to Jasper.

'Trevor. That's what Donald called him.' Jasper smirked at his nephew. The first stab.

'I did not!' Donald lunged back.

'Right. You two cut it out.' The sergeant turned back to Robert. 'Trevor. I've told you who I am. I'm a police officer and I have to investigate several crimes that have been committed, and you are a suspect.'

'Crimes?' Robert searched for a definition. He didn't like it. 'Trevor committed a crime? No.'

'Was it you who took money from the petrol station in Crompton Road? Was it you who attacked these two officers in the course of their duty? Was it you who stole the garage's tow truck? And was it you who destroyed a police patrol car and damaged several other vehicles whilst trying to avoid arrest?' Sergeant Billet was getting out of breath.

'My master's calling. I have only done what I have been instructed to do. It is that for which I am programmed.' Robert attempted to raise his head. Even a robot is uncomfortable talking from the floor. A further rocking movement in an effort to rise. Unsuccessful.

'Master? Now this sounds interesting. And who is your master, Trevor?' Sergeant Billet sensed a conclusion.

'Donald is my master.' Crisp and hardly tinny at all. It was almost as if Robert knew how damning this was.

Donald resorted to tears. He was only a little boy. He couldn't be blamed. Mummy!

Jasper suppressed a satisfying snort.

'Down the station with the lot of them. I think we can put this to bed, besides the statements that is.' Sergeant Billet could almost smell his pot of tea. 'Move them out, Harry.'

'And the junk on the floor?' Harry waved a hand over Robert, who wasn't sure what was going on. He only knew he needed a repair.

'Get the uncle to switch him off and bundle our metal friend in the boot of your car. Oh, no, we can't can we? Your car's in a worse state than this scrap. I'll need to talk to you about that.' Sergeant Billet needed a scapegoat.

Chapter Eight

Such unusual happenings and excitement was great news, and the goings-on the previous evening at Donald Clipper's house was all over Granford Manor School the next day. Michael couldn't believe it. Donald Clipper had made his own robot? Done all these things with it? Criminal things? What sort of machine had he built?

It was only natural that groups of children would descend on Michael. He was the robot builder. A hero at the school. Anything to do with robots, he would be the person to seek out.

Did you help him with the robot? Was it one of your designs? Did you give him yours? A battery of questions.

Michael was as baffled as the next kid. He couldn't help thinking about it all day. In class he was not paying attention and in Chemistry he was in trouble. Hardly a scrap of work. His mind was churning. Whirring away.

He headed home from school in a pack. Donald Clipper and the robot still the main topic of the huddled striding group. Michael, at the centre, bag slung over his shoulder, puzzled.

Gran was shuffling around the house and moaning. Nothing changed. Michael agreed with everything she said. It was how he dealt with her. There were greater concerns.

He fought the temptation for about an hour. But it was too strong. Clipper couldn't make his own robot. The kid was an idiot. Where could he have found such a machine? Michael had to check. Had to see if his robot, if Robert, was still in pieces in the attic. A dreadful thought was growing, like an expanding ink blot, in his mind.

Dust and grime lay as a sprinkling of grey snow on the dark shapes of the poorly lit loft space. So many boxes and bundles. Where to start? And with every examination, disappointment. Michael spent over three hours searching. Pulling out an assortment of rubbish and discarded paraphernalia. 'He's not here,' Michael muttered to himself. 'No sign of any part of that pesky robot.'

He gave himself a further half-hour and then gave up. Resigned to the worrying conclusion that there was an awfully strong possibility that Donald Clipper's robot was in fact Robert. And the significance of that was slowly sinking in. Crimes had been committed. Serious offences that this robot was being blamed for. How did he stand as the creator? Was he liable for Robert's behaviour?

After a fitful night's sleep where he was constantly bombarded with weird robot dreams, Michael decided he had to own up and confront his demons. A cursory look at the freshly delivered local newspaper left him with no alternative. Of course he would have the most difficult task of telling his parents the dreadful truth. His stomach ached and he could hardly breathe.

'A robot?' Michael's mother was dazed. 'You made a robot? Getting my brother Dan involved?' She didn't know whether to be proud or angry.

'I'm flabbergasted. It's incredible. It's damn well deceitful as well.' His dad was overspilling with conflicting emotions. 'Where is this robot? What did you say you called him, Robert?'

'Well that's the problem.' Michael bent his head, nearly to his knees.

'Problem? Now, my boy, I remember only too well that incident at the school a while ago with Squinch. A terrible episode that you weren't very truthful about.'

'It's not my fault,' Michael sniffled.

'So what is this problem?' his dad insisted.

Michael pulled out the copy of the *Thames Ditton Chronicle*, and shoved it under his father's severe face.

Michael watched his father's eyes scan every line,

and scour every picture. Front page stuff that continued inside. Not a story hidden between garage sales and the local craft society news. Shouting out Robert's appalling crimes in every detail. Smashed cars and a cleverly angled snap of the shattered showroom window.

'I don't get it,' Michael's father finally puffed. 'Your robot? How come?'

Mrs. Dobbins had retreated to the kitchen. A cup of tea was the only answer. This was too distressing.

'Stolen. Somehow Robert was stolen from the attic. I took him to pieces and hid him away up there.' Michael explained. 'I don't know how that Donald Clipper got hold of him, I really don't. Nothing to do with me.' Michael pleaded his innocence.

'What now, son?' A stern voice.

'I think I had...' Michael looked up at his father with spaniel eyes. '...*we* had, better go down the police station and help sort this out.

'Get your coat.' Mr. Dobbins was already on his feet.

Chapter Nine

Michael and his dad stood at the high wooden counter of the police station.

'Sergeant, Sergeant Billet.' The desk sergeant hailed his compatriot. 'Someone I think you might like to talk to.'

'Yep? And what can I do for you two?' Billet carried his mug of tea at his chest. Crumbs from two digestive biscuits clung to his tunic and the edge of his mouth. 'Busy time here. Hope it's important.'

'Bill Dobbins, and my son Michael.' A quick introduction. 'It's about the incident with the robot,' Michael's dad began.

'Robot? Who said anything about a ruddy robot?' Sergeant Billet was reddening at the cheeks.

'In the paper. All that destruction. A robbery. Assault. A crime spree they reported,' Mr. Dobbins continued.

'Certainly had that,' Billet agreed. 'But who said any flipping thing about a robot?'

'Well. I thought...wasn't it?' Mr. Dobbins was baffled.

'Very sensitive case this. Perhaps we need to talk out back. This way.' Sergeant Billet guided Mr.

Dobbins and Michael through to an interview room behind the front desk.

'Talk is, in the neighbourhood and at Michael's school, that all the damage and the crimes were committed by a *metal man*, a robot.' Mr. Dobbins endeavoured to explain.

'I see. So if that was so, how can you be of any assistance in this matter?' Sergeant Billet was sounding official.

Mr. Dobbins looked over at Michael, sucked in his cheeks. 'This is a little difficult.' Another peek at his son. 'You see. This robot...this robot...was.' A burst of courage. 'Was made by my son, Michael.' Words spat out, as if they tasted bad.

Sergeant Billet tapped his lips with his forefinger and eyed the two people in front of him. He'd sensed this case from the start was going to be a pain in the neck. 'So your son, Michael, sat there...' Billet pointed rudely. '...your son built a robot capable of all this mayhem and disaster? A complicated piece of machinery that caused havoc, on my patch?' The sergeant shook his head. 'Is it me or you, Mr. Dobbins, that is mad?'

'No, honestly, I did. I built Robert at home in the basement. My Gran was there, but she didn't know. No one knew. From bits and pieces and stuff from the shops in the high street. He was my friend.' Michael blurted.

'Nice try son.' Sergeant Billet sat back, smug. 'Robert eh? The robot we have in custody. Oh, I didn't mean to say that.' He looked towards the door to see if anyone may have heard. 'Anyway, the robot that is helping us with our enquiries goes by the name of Trevor. So there.'

'Trevor?' Michael quizzed.

'Look, we haven't finished here. I was about to tell you that this robot my son built was stored in pieces in our attic. It was obviously stolen and used by the villains responsible for the criminal rampage.' Mr. Dobbins hurried to enlighten the sergeant.

'So you're here to report a theft?' Sergeant Billet squinted. Things couldn't have got more complicated.

'No. We have come to perhaps throw some light on these quite bizarre events. Here to help the police,' Mr. Dobbins tried to explain.

If he didn't get a fresh brew of tea he'd go barmy. Sergeant Billet slumped in his chair. The whole thing was a nightmare.

'We don't appear to be achieving much do we?' Mr. Dobbins shrugged.

'Now, what I need to do is to investigate further. More enquiries needed. I would ask you to keep what has happened here to yourselves. I will be in contact. Statements and the like.' A hot cuppa was really calling. 'Thanks for popping in. It's been helpful.' Sergeant Billet was right fed up. He could imagine a mountain of paperwork rising from his desk. Straight forward, that's the way he liked it. None of this robot stuff. Too complicated.

Michael and his dad slid away, leaving the sergeant grunting under his breath and heading for the canteen.

'Robot my foot.' Gran had got hold of the story whilst they were at the police station. 'Whatever next? My word, we didn't have robots in the house when I was a girl. My father would never...'

Michael disappeared; her words drifting into the lounge. Off to the safety of his room. Gran never heard the *old bat* that he muttered at every stride up the stairs. It had been a sad day. He had thought Robert was tucked up in the attic. A robot just resting. Safe. But no, Robert was out robbing garages, stealing cars, causing untold damage. The past adventures were replayed in his sleep. Adventures with his old friend, Robert. Where was that goof now?

Robert came home sooner than Michael expected. Well, it was just a collection of metal pieces and tangled wire. In a box delivered to the house by van. A jumble that Sergeant Billet had spirited away.

It hadn't taken long for the Crown Prosecution Service to inform Billet of the impossibility of pressing charges against a mechanical object, and quite categorically that no one in their right mind was going to take a witness statement from a robot. Let alone produce one in court.

It had been agreed by all parties, including Michael's dad, that any reference to, or suggestion that, something made of household junk and bits of electrical scrap was capable of these hideous events was taboo. Hence the sudden arrival of Robert's parts.

'Where shall I put him?' Michael timidly asked his dad.

'What are we going to do with him is the point. Shove him in the basement I suppose. Like home I expect.'

'Thanks Dad.' Michael struggled to the top of the basement steps until a helping hand took most of the weight.

'In the corner.' A half smile on Mr. Dobbins' face. 'Going to put him together again, aren't you?'

'Can I?' Michael beamed.

'Strict conditions, son. No nonsense this time.' Mr. Dobbins couldn't hide his own enthusiasm.

'Will you help, Dad?' Michael wanted him involved even though he doubted his father's robot-building skills. Working together on the project would be bonding and help repair their fractured relationship. They both realised this.

Chapter Ten

It took Michael barely four days to rebuild Robert. Surprisingly his dad kept his word and was an eager assistant. Michael was even able to improve on his original design during the reconstruction. The greatest improvement being a series of hinges at Robert's knees that allowed his legs to bend.

'Robert will be pleased with these,' Michael told his dad as they screwed them in place.

'Running the hundred metres for Great Britain I'll bet.' A dad's joke.

'Robert's looking good. Don't you think, Dad?' Michael was so proud. All the old emotions filling his head.

'From the outside.' Mr. Dobbins put his arm round Michael's shoulder. 'Got to remember old chum, he's not your Robert inside. He's still Trevor.'

'Trevor. I'd forgotten. All the work here. Any ideas?' Michael sat forlornly. Suddenly saddened.

'You'll have to get Uncle Dan over. Didn't he program Robert initially?'

'Maybe I'll try him out first. The batteries are charged.' Michael couldn't wait.

'Be careful, son.' Mr. Dobbins was nervous yet

excited. This was all new ground for him. He watched as his son proceeded to operate the switch.

Not the dramatic resurrection that Mr. Dobbins had imagined. A slow shaking and metallic tinkle. Fingers twitching and the snapping of sparks from deep within. Robert was awakening. Just like any computer that's shut down in a hurry there were issues to complete, disks to check and memory to be activated. Robert's mechanism was going through these.

Michael and his father watched and waited.

'Hello, Robert.' Michael sensed it was time.

Robert set his camera eyes on the boy. There was a whirring of the focus. 'My name is Trevor.' It didn't feel right but it was the logical, programmed reply.

'Gently, son.' Mr. Dobbins was cautious.

'Don't you remember me?' Michael tapped his chest. 'I built you. We're friends.'

There were fizzes and buzzes from far down in Robert's insides. Deep humming and hisses.

'My name is Trevor. Donald is my master. My name is Trevor. My name is Trevor. My name is Trevor.' From a chant to a slow murmur. Smoke drifted from the hatch door in Robert's chest. Chips were in conflict, programs in dispute and a circuit somewhere was overheating. 'My...name...my...na...' Robert shut down with a thud.

'Uncle Dan, and now!' Mr. Dobbins wasn't going to let his son touch the ailing robot.

Reprogramming a robot isn't the easiest of tasks. And Uncle Dan was no expert. It took him hours, and then he wasn't certain he'd cracked it. 'Touch wood.' He shook his head and slapped the kitchen table as he left. 'Let me know how it goes.' A wing and a prayer and Robert would be okay. It was more hope than science.

Michael tucked in some leads and dislodged wires that his uncle had left protruding between joints. 'Let's have another go,' he said to his dad.

A loud whine announced that Robert was functioning. Some other sizzling noises seemed to pulsate through the metal body and gradually dwell on a low hum.

'Hello Robert.' Michael peered into the camera eyes, urging recognition.

Cobwebs cleared in the far recesses of the basic system that Uncle Dan had enabled. Dust dispersed. All the alien commands that Donald Clipper had initiated were blown away. As if following an old pathway, on familiar ground. 'Hello Master.' Robert proudly enunciated in pure metallic English.

It's a strange feeling, wanting to hug a piece of tin. But that's how Michael Dobbins felt. He just wanted to hold his friend in his arms. 'Robert.' Rolling tears and a quivering voice. He knew then that his robot was back and that there were going to be even more fantastic adventures ahead.

Robert was put to bed in his own territory. His own corner of the basement. No longer a hidden oddity. Now a member of the family. No shame. A proud resident in the Dobbins' household.

It wasn't long, however, before trouble with a capital M caught up with Robert.

A physics lesson for Michael at school. Testing which materials were magnetic. *Test ten different items, made of a variety of materials in the home.* Cinch of a homework for Michael Dobbins, and he knew exactly what he would attach his horseshoe magnet to. It would be such a whizz sticking it all over his friend, Robert.

'And now the other hand.' Robert was a trusting guinea pig. He sat as if he was receiving a manicure. 'Some fingers are and some are not,' Michael announced.

'Not what?' Robert's crisp enquiry.

'Magnetism, Robert. I am testing to see how much of you is magnetic. See.' Michael slapped his magnet against Robert's bucket head. 'Attraction. That's what they call it. Sticks to you. Means you are steel there. But these fingers.' Michael returned to the huge hands that he had been testing. 'The fingers made from old cigar tubes, they're aluminium and therefore not attracted.' Michael repeated some of the tripe that 'Froggy' Francis, the science teacher, had prattled on about in double physics that afternoon. 'From the biscuit tins you clatter around on, to your bucket brain, Robert, you are very attractive.' Michael chortled at his own joke.

Robert tried hard to imitate the laugh. It came out as if a vacuum cleaner was picking up a pile of nails that rattled up the suction pipe.

'Here you go.' Michael threw his school magnet onto Robert's chest. 'I'm off for some tea.'

Robert pushed the magnet all over the mucky dustbin; his rough and rusting shell. Sure enough the little limpet stayed glued to his tinny body in all the places he thrust the scratching red horseshoe.

There are magnets **AND** there are **MAGNETS**.

Mr. Dobbins was proud of his son's robot and looking for any excuse to show him off. But, if he had really understood the nature of Robert, and his ability to make a disaster out of an ordinary situation, he wouldn't have been so eager to include Robert on this excursion.

'I'm just taking him along to get something for the car. It's all right, isn't it, son?' His father's face beamed.

Michael wasn't so sure. But he couldn't disappoint

that blazing smile. Couldn't take away that fizzling pride. Seemed harmless enough. But then it always did.

Except that Mr. Dobbins' bone-shaker wasn't the newest of motors and spare parts for that heap were only found in 'graveyards', where they butchered such junk. Transplanted any saveable bits for a couple of quid. Self-service. You had to climb cars, that were piled, piggy-backed, on the crumpled roof of each other. Four-high in places. Stacked, swaying and sadly past their prime.

'Up there, Robert.' Mr. Dobbins indicated to his front seat passenger. A metal dummy man as it appeared to the guys working in the yard. But clearly a friend. 'Ford Escort. Same blue.' He tapped the side of his door through the open window.

Robert focussed. Saw the pile of cars lean precariously in the gusting wind. 'Robots not working.' Robert spoke slow and deliberate. 'Dead robots.'

'Just cars. Like the one you are in.' Mr. Dobbins explained.

Robert had wanted to be a car himself, when he initially saw them on his adventure with Michael. His first day out.

'Robert still sad.' Soft metal tone. A brushed aluminium voice.

'You stay here while I see if I can get that boot

lid. Looks sound enough. This one's had it.' Mr. Dobbins pointed behind him. 'Corrosion, Robert. Thing you have to watch out for, eh?' Mr. Dobbins rolled his head. It didn't seem odd to joke with a robot.

Robert watched as his master's father attempted to scramble up the jagged metal. He managed to reach the roof of an old Vauxhall Victor and was swinging on the flapping door of a crushed and pilfered Standard Vanguard. Not much of a mountain climber was Bill Dobbins. Stuck at base camp. He wasn't going to make the summit. Above him the Escort boot lid wobbled as if to celebrate its victory. 'Damn!'

Robots don't act as you expect them to. Especially Robert. He sensed Mr. Dobbins' aborted mission and was prompted into action. It was only natural to assist. To his left was the final solution. Cars were squashed between the scrunching power of massive hydraulic blades. A neat cube of entrails. Blocks easily stacked. Lifted on to the backs of lorries by the adhering ring of an electro-magnet. Robert recognised the pull. Knew all about magnetic attraction. A simple resolution.

It was operated by buttons on a long, swinging lead attached to the rail along which the magnet ran. And it ran well into the area where the stack of corpse motors were heaped in grotesque rows. A vulgar Stonehenge.

And the operator, a man not known for his bravery. Who wasn't going to be *no martyr*. *If the iron man wants the controls he can have them*. One more deserter.

Robert fingered the buttons until he saw the grubby ring descending towards him. One more push and he was flung with a hollow *klunk* into the awesome pulling power of the magnetic field.

Mr. Dobbins, marooned on the roof of the Vauxhall Victor, heard the magnet suck up a tin can. An abrupt *chonk*. Saw Robert held firm. Legs waving. Arms wrestling with the control lead. 'My goodness! Oh dear!' He wasn't at all used to the crazy antics of Michael's robot. 'What is he going to do?' A voice verging on panic.

Robert was quite enjoying just dangling there. But he had a mission. Gritty scraping and a low growl announced movement of his 'cable car'. Deliberately and with purpose Robert was trundled across the scrapyard along the rail-track beam. Hanging, with arms spread in front and trailing legs. Robert *was* Metallicman. In the dull light of the yard he floated. A rattling superhero about to save the world.

'What are you doing?' Mr. Dobbins, nervously clutching the swaying door, shouted at the approaching robot. 'You're going to kill me!' Blustering then screaming. Fear becoming panic.

'Worry not, I will get your boot.' Robert's knightly, but tinny voice was drowned by the whine of the travelling magnet, now increasing in pace.

Mr. Dobbins watched Robert's trailing legs disappear behind the high rise of cars above his head. An aircraft behind a building. The pile of cars rocked and threatened to topple. Mr. Dobbins held on for his life. Clawing at the dangling Vanguard door.

Robert had plucked the whole car, the blue Ford Escort, from the top of the heap. And where it had been attached to the other crumpled cars, it tore and split, scratched and scraped as it was lifted away.

Robert clutched the car firmly and rode it for another fifty metres or so, before lowering it to the ground. Well, it was like lowered, only with more use of gravity than mechanics. It fell with an almighty crunch and kicked up a cloud of choking dust from a barren area of the yard.

Robert fell with the remnants of the automobile. Spread out on the roof. A star formed of metal limbs extended to their limit.

'I have your boot.' Robert made his announcement to the shivering wreck that was Mr. Dobbins. Now huddled low and cuddling the rear wheel of the Vanguard.

Robert held out the piece of metal he had torn from the smashed car. More than just a few dents from its travels. The vertical journey being the most destructive. 'Robert doesn't think it will fit you. Do you not need two?' Robert was now thrusting the boot lid at the trembling face of Mr. Dobbins. 'Do not boots come in pairs?' Robert quizzed the frightened man.

'Not a bb...ooo...tt you wear. It's a c...aaa...rr boooot.' Mr. Dobbins tried to explain through shaking lips. 'For my c...aaa...r. Yes, for my car.' Perhaps it was all a dream. Mr. Dobbins was in shock. He jabbered and mumbled. A very scared individual.

It took three employees, burly and tattooed, from the scrapyard to rescue the devastated man from the roof of the Vauxhall Victor.

'Them cars are stacked for a reason, guv'nor. Ain't safe your mate removing them. Specially the blooming top one. And 'im usin' company equipment. Now get out of 'ere and don't you and that idiot in the tin suit come back. You got it?' The foreman rubbed his hands together as if to remove dirt. They were filthy anyway. A pointless activity.

Mr. Dobbins just nodded. This was a nightmare, from which he couldn't wake up.

'The boot?' Robert's chirpy metallic voice triumphantly questioned. It was the prize. 'Where will it go?' Totally unaware of the chaos he had caused. The lump of car he proudly held on to, and offered to the slumped man, was rippled and bent, twisted and scrunched, scratched and worthless. It could have been any part of a car. Any part of anything made of sheet steel.

Michael listened to his shattered father relate the story over a hot cup of tea. Robert was in disgrace. It was an embarrassment all round. There had been many occasions before, but this one was different. Robert was a welcomed guest in the Dobbins' household. No longer the fugitive in the basement. But for the moment his power was off and he stood in his corner, still clutching the contorted scrap of metal that he had valiantly snatched for his master's father.

'I'm sure he meant well, Dad.' Michael pleaded for his friend. 'No intention of being a nuisance. Probably misunderstood the situation.' Excuses rattling out.

'Your father's in no mood to discuss the matter.' Mrs. Dobbins was concerned about her husband's condition. Protective and tending.

'Robots? Whatever next. Thought there'd be trouble. Went through the war without a flipping robot we did. And we 'ad it 'ard. I can tell you.' Gran was rambling as she waddled back into the kitchen for a refill, finger jabbing at imaginary enemies.

Dust and distrust. Robert was left idle in his dark

dungeon. Punishment. Michael never visited. His father was slowly recovering from his ordeal at the junkyard, and Michael was aware not to aggravate the mental injury. Hopefully things would be back to normal pretty soon.

Chapter Eleven

Well, everything seemed normal when Michael yanked at the basement door and cast the first light on his robot for over two months. They don't move. Robots without power stay very still. Good as gold. Rather grubby and dressed in cobwebs, but no trouble at all. If only that's how it remained.

Robert seemed so peaceful. So harmless and pathetic. Michael dusted him down and flicked off some rather dubious droppings that sat on his shoulder.

'You need a good clean.' Michael wandered around his statue friend. 'Probably some oil and a few fuses no doubt. And definitely a mighty charge in those batteries. They're certain to be flat.'

He spent the morning polishing and preening the outer shell of Robert. Two thick cables fed into his chest cavity, bringing voltage life blood. But it was just maintenance. No impending activity intended.

Except, there was one little job that Michael had been asked to do where Robert could be a great help. Nothing difficult. No real chance of a mishap. Just a brief excursion; a simple task. 'Be all right. Couldn't possibly be a problem.' Michael nattered to himself.

'Not like with Dad. This is my robot. I can make things go smoothly.' He was convincing himself.

'We're off to the Do-It-Yourself or DIY store, Robert.' Michael stood squarely in front of his robot. 'No monkey business, do you understand?'

Freshly awoken, Robert was all fuzzy inside. You can't start a complicated piece of electronics and expect everything to register. Settings being updated and systems being analysed. Programs run and data verified.

'You do understand, don't you, Robert.' Michael was concerned about the lack of communication.

'Yes, Master.' A standard reply now in the data base. Robert continued to fizz and pulsate, crackle and hiss. 'DIY store. Yes, Do-It-Yourself.' Research engines churned within to throw up the records. 'Do-It-Yourself.' A brisk and crisp response. Robert was receiving information. It wasn't quite the same information that was running through Michael's head.

It was just like old times walking along the pavement with Robert. Except now Robert didn't march like a Russian soldier. With his new knee joints his legs were able to bend with extraordinary flexibility. Even human knees are only capable of a hinge movement. Robert's didn't have the restrictions of complicated ligament arrangements and so his lower leg swung comically back and forth, producing an exaggerated step at each stride. A very silly walk indeed.

'Now, listen to me carefully.' Michael began to caution Robert as they strode towards the industrial estate where the store was situated. 'There are many dangerous items in this place. The sort of stuff you could cause a lot of damage with. Only touch the things I tell you to. Understand?' Michael was taking no chances.

'Robert understands.' Firm agreement. Plenty of echo but no crackle. Even Robert recalled with pleasure those days when he accompanied his master on some splendid adventures. 'Only what you tell me,' he assured Michael. There was no way he wanted to get into trouble again. He never really understood what had gone wrong. Only that people shouted and weren't at all happy with Robert. Today would be different.

Some hope!

'Get me a trolley, Robert.' Michael pulled out a list that his mother had given him. Decorating stuff. A gift for his father. A reminder of the bedrooms that he had begun an age ago and remained unfinished. 'Get one from that rack over there.' He pointed his robot in the direction of a neat row of shopping carts snaking along a boundary fence. A new arrangement. Chained and demanding a pound coin to be released.

Too many had been dumped around the car park, left by the roadside or found their way into the nearby brook.

Robert tugged at the end trolley. It resisted. The connected rank wobbled and twisted. Robert jerked at the handle again. Still they held on. No coin, no trolley.

Michael, standing near the entrance, ran his finger down the list, unaware of the trouble Robert was having or the mayhem it was going to cause.

Robert was aware that just one trolley was not being released. As if these metal, wheeled baskets were being awkward. Making his task unnecessarily difficult. Even a conspiracy. Robert yanked aggressively at the culprit trolley. All the chains between the carts were pulled taut. The chain attached to the first trolley held. Clanking out its defiance. But along the line, about half way down, a weaker link succumbed to the violent tugging and the snake was separated. Robert had his trolley. His trolleys! Sixteen in all. A weaving line that he wheeled back towards Michael. A short yet eventful journey. No matter how hard Robert attempted to keep the trolleys following a straight course, they proved disobedient. Even a robot's computer thought and control process isn't capable of taming a scything row of swinging shopping carts. They had a mind of their own.

Other customers were returning to their cars. Some laden with cumbersome loads. A Wednesday. Senior Citizens ten percent discount. Unwitting victims lacking awareness and agility. The first casualty fought with a maverick trolley carrying loft insulation and boarding. Pulling to the left, one wheel sticking. A cursing driver struggling as best he could forward. Robert's mowing line of trolleys caught the side of the man's load. Removing the cart from his grip, carrying it sideways, toppling and scattering the cargo amongst other parked vehicles. The elderly man stood with his hands in front of him, clutching an imaginary handle, shaking. Eyes wide, mouth wide. Spectacles lopsided. A distant gurgling noise from somewhere deep down in his throat.

After the impact Robert's trolley caravan swung viciously to the right. A whipping action. Another direct hit. This time emulsion paint in large tins carried precariously by a tradesman. A burly fellow. Popeye arms and the last fraction of a roll-up cigarette hanging from his lips. Someone who didn't stand for any nonsense.

Not every paint tin spilled. Some merely rolled and lodged behind wheels of parked cars. But enough emptied from the wreck for there to be a sheet of brilliant white thrown across the car park. A tidal wave of paint spilled into the path of other shoppers, and pond around cars to leave them as unreachable islands in a milky ocean.

'What the bleeding 'ell?' snorted the vexed tradesman. 'Knock me flipping paint over? Come 'ere.'

Michael, and everyone within a hundred metres, became suddenly aware of trouble. A mean and hostile explosion of a voice.

Robert clung on to his trolleys. He was nearly at the entrance where Michael waited. He had registered the unpleasantness of the irate workman.

'I said come 'ere. Aluminium man. Yes, you with the funny suit on. Get over 'ere and clear this lot up and get me some more emulsion. Now!' He was a man incensed and getting madder. Bulldog expression and a menacing posture. Crouched like a gorilla.

Robert continued his journey, unaware of the chaos he had caused. Knowing only that a man was shouting. Aiming his anger at him.

'When I says come 'ere I means it.' Robert's arm was grabbed and held firm. 'Now I wants you to sort this lot out. Knocked all me stuff over without a word of apology. I don't likes that sort of manner. No, I ain't puttin' up with that.' A grimace and baring of teeth.

Robert knew how to perform. Billy Carter was a similar problem. Even the two policemen, dealt with whilst he was under Donald Clipper's influence, remained in the memory bank.

Flapping like a hooked pike. The agitated decorator blustered and puffed. Crimson in the face and blue at the lips. Robert hoisted him high and wide. Swinging him so that his legs spread and his arms groped thin air.

'Oi! Let me down. I'll...bleeding have your...guts for garters, I...will.' Gasping threats from the struggling tradesman.

Michael was now at Robert's side. He could see the disaster zone. Knew he'd made the same mistake. 'You've done it again. I said *no* trouble.'

'I have the trouble.' Robert bounced the man up and down a couple of times. His shirt split a little. Robert tucked his fingers under the swaying man's braces, who dipped and rose as if a yo-yo. 'Robert will deal with the trouble.'

'The trouble is you.' Michael was exasperated. 'You have to let him go.'

'Yeah. You have...to let...me go.' Brave words from the pendulum man.

Robert gave him a last shake and brought him down to his level. Face to face. And then let him slip to the floor. He slithered away like a startled grass snake. No appetite for confrontation now.

Michael dragged his robot away from the trolley rank and pushed him into the store. Back in the car park the milky paint was disappearing down the drains or hardening around the wheels of long term parked cars. Arcing white tyre marks drew the escape routes of other customers. There was no sign of the tradesman, so sorely wronged, loud and angry. You don't survive an encounter with Robert unscathed.

'I should have known better. Robert, you've done it again.' Michael couldn't hide his distress. Stomping to a quiet part of the store.

'Robert was only dealing with the trouble.' A mild, tinny explanation. A little confused about his reception. He was certain he had acted in the proper manner. It was obvious that some thought processes were beyond a computer.

'Did you see that old guy after you rammed his trolley? The man was a wreck. And that rough bloke with the paint. Hanging him up in the air. Paint all over the car park. Let's hope Dad doesn't get a bill for that. What am I going to do with you?' Michael spoke through his teeth. Fizzing words closely aimed at Robert, but an attempt to keep his fury out of range of other shoppers.

Robert was confused. 'Trying to help, Master.' An innocent steely voice.

'Yeah. Some help.' Michael didn't look up. Again he studied his list. 'Let's get this shopping and get out of here. Filler. Now where is that?'

Robert followed close behind. He wasn't going to make a false move. He'd been dismantled before. He didn't want that happening again. However, as Michael marched towards the aisle he needed, Robert was stopped in his tracks.

'Catch up. Stop dawdling. Get here, Robert.' Michael waved an arm at his robot. 'What are you looking at?'

Robert didn't move. Stuck to the spot. Couldn't take his eyes off a large gleaming display. All sorts. Bright and handsome. A collection of the latest dustbins. A new body! Wouldn't he look smart with a gleaming dustbin body instead of his tatty old thing, he thought. Robert put out an exploring finger to feel the smoothness of the shining galvanised dustbin. Closer in, with his plastic nose nearly touching the bin he could almost see his reflection.

'What's holding you up?' Michael had returned to see why Robert had stopped.

'New bodies. Look Master. Robert would like a new body.' Robert spoke to Michael without looking at him. He couldn't take his eyes off the sparkling dustbins.

'No chance! Come on there's work to do.' Michael wasn't feeling in a generous mood, and anyway he couldn't possibly afford the twenty pounds they were asking. And there was too much work involved in transferring all the electronics of his robot. 'Now let's get that filler.'

Michael marched off. His patience with Robert was wearing thin.

'Ah, here's the filler.' Michael stood on his toes to reach the packet high on a shelf. 'Can't quite get the thing. Robert, give me a hand, I've pushed it further back. Robert? Robert, where are you? Oh, no, he's disappeared again.'

Robert had willingly followed Michael, and almost kept up with him until he reached the filler. If it hadn't been for the paint display. His legs wouldn't carry him past that. Cans of all colours. Bright new paint pots stacked high and wide. Just the right sizes for a new set of arms and legs. 'Mmmm.' Robert was mesmerised. He had thought all paint tins were like the ones he had been built with; scruffy, dented and with hardened paint drips stuck to the sides. Like solidified lava.

'No! not those either.' Michael grabbed hold of Robert's arm. He read the robot's mind. 'No new body, no new legs and no new arms. You're staying just as you are. Now, get here.'

Michael didn't take his eyes off Robert for the rest of the shopping trip. Making certain the robot was ahead of him at all times. Robert did falter by the shelf cluttered with colourful buckets, but was quick to realise Michael would chase him clear. Anyway he wasn't so impressed with having a plastic head.

Michael eventually had all the items on his list. Robert was frog-marched to the checkout. There was a welcoming party waiting. Arms folded and with a grim face stood the grey-suited store manager, Cecil Spinks. On each side two henchmen, the store name emblazoned on their dark blue shirts. Their arms similarly folded. Snarling faces.

'Just a minute, sir. Need to have a word with you.' The group surrounded Robert. 'If you would step this way.' Half a smile from the ambushing store manager.

Michael was sidelined as Robert was led into an office. They had their offender. No need for the boy. Michael panicked. Threw the cash at the checkout girl and scarpered. Legged it home.

'I haven't called the police as yet, Mister?' Cecil Spinks leaned forward, head turned. His ear in Robert's face. 'Your name?'

'My name is Robert.' Stainless steel ring with every syllable.

'Well Mr. Robert, as I have said, there's been no call to the police as yet, but if we can't sort this out I will be on to them immediately.'

'Sort this out?' Robert was baffled.

'Shall we drop all the funny stuff to start with. It'll only complicate matters if you continue to wear that odd suit. I can tell you it isn't a good advertisement for this store, you wearing all that rubbish. I trust this is not a deliberate attempt to damage the reputation of Grumleys DIY. Not from our competitors are you? Some sort of sabotage expedition?'

'Suit, sabotage?' Robert waited to retrieve the data.

'Come on, sir, the suit. You can leave it over here and take it with you once we have discussed the incidents in the car park.'

'I have no suit.' Robert had the information. 'Robert does not wear clothes.' Defiant metallic voice.

'Look, if you're going to play games then this will get serious. You've damaged property, assaulted shoppers and left my car park looking like a flock of albatrosses have been using it for bombing practice.'

Robert didn't flinch. He was searching for albatross in his memory bank but couldn't relate one to bombing.

'Help the gentleman with his fancy dress, boys.' Cecil Spinks instructed his assistants.

The four goons grasped Robert's arms and legs. 'Blooming heck! It ain't no suit. He's made of metal. Waste stuff, but it's all metal!' One squeaked. They all stepped back.

'You sure?' Cecil quizzed.

'Yeah. You feel.'

Cecil Spinks tapped Robert's arm, then his leg and then gave a series of raps all over his body. 'Blow me.' He sat back, flabbergasted.

'I am a robot.' Robert proudly announced. Speaking out for the metallic minority.

'Call the Bill, Jimmy.' Cecil Spinks knew he was out of his depths. 'We'll see about this robot fellow.'

Cecil went out to greet the arriving police car. No sirens or blue lights flashing. It wasn't serious crime or their tea break.

'You can see the car park for yourself.' Cecil pointed out the large area of what looked like spilled milk. 'And I have the names and addresses of the people who have suffered at the hands of this villain.'

Cecil marched the two policemen towards the office where Robert stood. A slight humming from his computer, but no real movement. 'This isn't quite the normal case, officer,' the store manager began to explain, 'our culprit isn't one of your run-of-the-mill shoppers.' Cecil Spinks was finding it difficult to fully explain.

'Blooming heck!' PC Harry Evans wobbled on his porky legs. 'Oh no!'

'I don't believe it!' Pete stopped in his tracks, mouth wide open.

'What's wrong?' Cecil Spinks asked. 'What is the matter?' He was alarmed at the police officers' reactions.

'It's flipping Trevor the bleeding robot, that's what's wrong.'

'My name is Robert.' The policemen were corrected by a stern iron voice.

'Whatever your ruddy name is, it's still you!' Harry Evans couldn't believe his bad luck.

'You know this er...person?' Cecil enquired.

'That ain't no person, that's one flipping chunk of metal, and one flipping chunk of trouble.' Pete explained.

'So this is a robot?' Cecil Spinks wanted confirmation.

'Yep.' Harry sighed, pulled off his cap and perched his large bottom on the nearest chair. 'What's he done now?'

Cecil described in emotional detail Robert's latest misdemeanours. 'Can I hand this over to you now?' he concluded.

Harry scratched his scalp and sighed again. 'Mr. Spinks, I'm sorry to say that we have some difficulty here. As you have been informed, this piece of metal.' He jabbed a finger at Robert. 'This piece of metal ain't a human, he's a bleeding robot. Nothing in law that allows you to prosecute a lump of tin. Not to mention the embarrassment all round. My advice to you is to forget pursuing this matter, and do your best to cover it up with head office. Be for the best, I can assure you.' Harry fiddled with his cap.

Cecil looked at Pete for support. Almost tearful eyes from the store manager.

'He's right. Ruddy robot gets away with it. You should see what he's done in the past.' Pete touched his cheek, remembering the harsh twigs from the hedge.

Robert was escorted out of the building by the store heavies. A little less bravado now. He made his way home with a jaunty stride. He wasn't in trouble at all.

Michael questioned Robert for an hour. 'They let you go? Said nothing would happen? You sure? You wrecked the car park, upset senior citizens, hung a wallpaper hanger up by his braces and destroyed a row of trolleys. And they're taking no action?'

'No trouble, Master.' Robert stood majestically erect. No one so innocent.

'Hmm, I'm not so sure. With all that havoc you caused I would have expected they'd call the police and have you arrested.'

'Police came to see me,' Robert nobly acknowledged. 'Nothing in the law that allows you to prosecute a piece of tin.' Robert crisply repeated Harry Evan's words. Same sanctimonious body language. He didn't fully understand the disparaging reference to tin.

'A lucky escape. Goodnight, Robert.' It wasn't quite as bad as Michael had imagined. With a click Robert was asleep.

Chapter Twelve

Whether out of caution or simply lack of opportunity Robert was left in the basement for a long time. Of course he didn't know that. Once the power was off he could hibernate all winter for all he knew. No electricity, no brain activity. No dreams in that long sleep.

Everybody's life was going well. Michael was proving a good student, and his father had recovered from his unfortunate experience. It was easy to forget the troublesome robot.

Until.

'Dad!' Michael threw his schoolbag to the floor and hunted for his father. 'Dad?'

'What is it?' Mr. Dobbins stepped through the French windows, muddy hands and gumboots.

'School sports day on Wednesday. They've got a father's race.'

Mr. Dobbins pulled a pained expression. 'You know how my ankle is since...well you know...getting the car part. I don't think I could manage it, son.' He hopped on one leg to demonstrate his injury.

'But, I've told the other kids how good you are. You'd win it hands down.'

'Sorry, son.' Mr. Dobbins slipped back into the garden.

Michael shoved the newssheet from school onto the dining room table, and made a surly ascent to his room. He wasn't happy. He knew his father was faster than all the other podgy parents. Fat bellies and smokers' coughs. It was a serious business amongst his peers. Bets had been made. Small things like magazines and computer games, DVDs and model stuff.

Michael hadn't the stomach for tea and excused himself in order to mope about in his bedroom.

Then it dawned.

Granford Manor School, being ever so politically correct, had worded the invitation for the Dad's Race to include other male adults. Too many one-parent families in the neighbourhood not to.

Robert was male and adult. And with his new hinged legs, Robert was fast. He'd show his father and the guys at school that his *other male adult* was supersonic.

Sometimes when you're out to prove something and you only see straight ahead of you, there's a tendency to forget the dangers. Michael was in that frame of mind, and all the mishaps and disasters that his *other male adult*, Robert, had created were conveniently forgotten.

'We have to practise.' Michael had his robot throbbing with power and was brushing off some of the dust that had accumulated. 'Do you understand?'

Robert was listening. Enjoying his valet. 'Robert understands.' Clear tin-can diction.

'Running, Robert. As fast as you can. The course is a hundred metres long. It's a race.' Michael rabbited away as he polished Robert's bucket head.

Robert entered the details into his search facility in order to get it crystal clear. Michael may have forgotten the cockups in the past, but Robert had them all stored on his hard disc. No mistakes this time. Robert was determined.

'There.' Michael stood back to examine his work. 'You'll do,' he decided. 'Now we need to train you without the other kids seeing us. I reckon we should go to the far end of the football field as it gets dark and see how you perform.'

At every corner Michael checked for spies. He was sure there would be other kids out with their overweight adults getting them fit for the contest. Tugging flabby dads along for some serious fitness exercises. When you're betting on a horse you need to make sure it reaches its peak at the right time.

There was only one woman and her dog where Robert was to show his paces. And she quickly fled. The fading light made Robert even more scary than normal.

'I've got my watch and I'm going to time you,' Michael explained. 'You have to run from here.' Michael pointed to the ground. 'To where I will be standing. Do you understand?' As if speaking to an idiot. 'Fast as you can. And don't start until I say so.'

'Yes, Master. Robert understands. Fast as he can.'

Michael was making his way to a point he reckoned was the right distance away, adjusting his watch as he went. He paused to struggle with the annoying little knob at the side which allows you to move the hands. They are always a pain.

Clunk!

Michael was thrown forward, sprawled on the floor. Robert stood looking down at him.

'What are you doing?' Michael spluttered.

'Robert ran as fast as he could to where you were standing,' he boastfully announced.

'You knocked me over.'

'Robert ran to exactly where you were standing,' Robert explained.

'I meant where I would be standing. I hadn't got there, had I? And you aren't meant to run into me. When did I say start? You buffoon!' The practice session hadn't begun well. 'Now.' Michael coughed out some grass still stuck in the corner of his mouth. 'I'm going up there.' He pointed to a goalpost. 'When I shout GO you start running. Not before. And not into me. Get it right this time.'

'GO!'

Very like a washing machine where the load is uneven and the balance out. It grumbles and clanks, jumps and rattles. That was how Robert ran. High lifting legs swinging wildly. No style. Hilariously cavorting across the dusky playing field like some alien warrior programmed to attack.

'Blow me down. Seven seconds or thereabouts.' Michael was astonished. That was a new world record wasn't it? 'Gee, that was fast. Maybe I got it wrong? Difficult to time on this.' He tapped the face of his watch. 'Go back to where you started, Robert. Let's do it again.' Michael fiddled with his timepiece. Thrusting it to his ear between a couple of shakes to make sure it was ticking.

'Go!'

Robert thundered down the same course; flailing piston legs. A metal bin full of shrapnel, hurtling, crankling and clatterbanking along. Fearsome sprinting.

'Seven seconds!' Michael scratched his head. 'I knew you'd be fast, but this is great.'

'Robert did well? Master pleased?' Not at all breathless. Well, without lungs you wouldn't be, would you?

'Fantastic. We're made. You are going to be the

star of school sports day, Robert.' Michael hugged his robot.

He would certainly be the star all right!

Squinch had left the school. He had never recovered from his encounter with Robert. Talk was that he had headed for a small island off the coast of Scotland. Teaching at a small primary school where no one built robots.

The new head was a small, inoffensive chap named Quentin Marigold. As you can imagine there were a variety of nicknames abounding. He wore the teacher's uniform, tweed suit with leather elbow patches, brown suede shoes, crumpled tie and milk bottle glasses. A subdued, shy man. Quite unlike his predecessor.

Sports day at Granford Manor School was chaotic at the best of times, but with Marigold trying to hold it together this year it degenerated into pandemonium.

The Fathers' Race was held last. After an assortment of plump mothers had tottered along with more wobble than pace. Several sprawling along the track as they attempted to break into a dash. An collection of inappropriate underwear on full display. Beached whales. An exhibition that delighted the children. Kids love nothing better than when adults make plonkers of themselves. The avenue of faces couldn't withhold their laughter. A good number doubled over in hysterics.

'*Last event. The fathers' race. Or rather, adult male,*' sports master Leonard Climp announced over the loudspeaker, correcting himself in time.

At once men dotted throughout the hub of spectators began removing tracksuits and running on the spot, shrugging shoulders and stretching. Some evidence of competition was emerging. They drifted to the start with more exercises on the way. Eyeing each other. Reckoning on their chances. Pupils who had bets were flitting around, checking on their 'horses'.

At the line the headmaster was allocating lanes. More trotting around and some sneering at other contestants. This was getting serious.

Michael led Robert to the start from behind the school buildings. Just a short walk that cut out the mass of parents.

'Just a minute. 'e ain't running in this race, is 'e?' A burly male adult enquired with a snarl. Ted Carter needed every advantage going.

'Yeah. We ain't running against the ruddy tin man.' Another equally unpleasant parent chirped in.

'Now, now,' pleaded Mr. Marigold, 'merely a matter of costume. Let's not get heated. Only a fun race.' Marigold twitched. He disliked aggravation of any sort. Being extremely short-sighted kept him oblivious to the nature of the new adult male entrant.

'Not to worry Gaz, we'll beat the iron maiden,' the first man gloated.

'So long as 'e don't use WD40, Ted.' Both men chortled. Another few attempts at touching toes and a jiggle of bottoms. The line of athletes was getting restless.

'Marks...set...' Quentin Marigold's shrill whistle followed.

Several men broke early. Marigold didn't have the nerve to call them back, despite cries of false start emitting from wives and girlfriends.

A buffalo charge. Stampeding male adults looking for glory. Storming, thrashing beasts. No prisoners.

Early jostling became violent sabotage. No quarter given. Speedier runners were nudged aside or bundled to the ground by hostile, lumbering contestants. A scramble for the finishing line. A delicate thread of cotton held by two small girls. Fear in their eyes.

Michael searched for Robert's progress. Where was he? Nowhere in the pack. A scrum trundling forward. Robert was absent. Stuck stationary on the start line. The other competitors were a quarter of the way home.

'Go!' Michael's urgent cry. How stupid of him. Robert was far too objective at times. He should have realised.

His long, gangling legs sprung into action. High lifting paint tins clattering behind the other runners. A huge step eating up the track. Robert was soon amongst them and ready to overshadow their struggling motion. And as quickly, flung to the ground. Ted Carter's stumpy leg extended to knock the robot from his stride. *No bleeding lump of steel was goin't' make a mockery out of 'im.*

Robert gouged a furrow in the soft ground as he fell. Again the charging horde pulled away. With a spring he pushed himself to his feet; catapulted away leaving a biscuit tin foot embedded in the turf. Dragging loose wires yet bounding ahead, and immediately in front of Ted Carter who had now resorted to tripping his mate, Gaz. His beaming face turned to puffed red anger when he knew he was riding pillion to a dustbin. Ted made a grab for the wretched metal man. A half-hearted rugby tackle that took the skin off the palms of his hands and left him grasping thin air. Stumbling into a lardy pile, feet before the finish line and in front of the whole school population and relatives.

Robert's victory was greeted with a huge cheer. A popular winner. Ever since the episode with Squinch, Robert had been the kids' hero. Now he had outrun a motley crew of flabby dads, bent on chicanery, he was fast becoming a legend at Granford Manor School.

And no trouble. Michael was elated. His robot had won the *adult male* race despite all kinds of trickery, and he hadn't caused an ounce of trouble. Great!

There were others, just a few, who saw it different. 'Seen wot he done to my Ted.' Mrs. Carter had been humiliated. 'Shouldn't 'ave been allowed.' She gabbled to an avenue of spectators whilst supporting her dazed husband's arm, as she and Billy led him away. A losing gladiator. Sour in defeat.

Chapter Thirteen

Minor repairs, that was all. A biscuit tin lost in the heat of tournament. No big deal. A robot to be proud of. Perhaps this would be the beginning of a trouble-free future for Michael and his great friend, Robert.

Unfortunately this would have been too simple, too easy.

Donald Clipper and his ghastly Uncle Jasper were never charged with an offence. Police and lawyers looked long and hard to find a path to prosecution, only to be dogged by the inevitable. These crimes were committed by a machine. A rusting scoundrel robot.

Now the fiendish pair were back at Donald's house. Reunited in a flimsy sense. Comrades in crime. No real bond except their one uniting emotion. Revenge!

'Betrayal.' Donald sat at the living room table. 'That's what it was. That ugly piece of waste metal betrayed me.'

'Us, dear nephew. We were both made to suffer because of that treason. I built him with these hands.' Jasper's saliva spilt into the hands he was looking down at. His demented head swaying from side to side.

'And now he is going to pay.' Donald trembled with anger.

'How? How are we to do that, my dear boy?' Jasper cackled.

'Destroy him! That is how.' Donald's eyes lit with a biting hatred.

'Destroy? What have you in mind.' Jasper drooled. Eager shunting movements with his legs.

'We build a robot of our own. A terrible beast. A killer robot!' Donald almost jumped from his chair. 'And with this despicable construction we exterminate that Judas, Robert.'

'Our own robot?' Jasper was taking it in slowly. 'One to obliterate the betrayer. Yes. Splendid plan.' Jasper sprung up. 'But, how?' And almost sank back in his seat.

'You. You can build such a brute. You've built one before. But, this time he will be massive and unstoppable. A servant to my wishes. Truly on my side. There will be no deception from our new creation. A monster to my specifications.' Donald announced, his teeth bared.

'I can do it.' Jasper was now convincing himself. 'A giant robot of enormous strength. I see it clearly. Have no worries, you will have your titanic ogre. An evil creature mechanically refined and electronically incomparable. My mind is to it already.' Jasper's lips quivered, and glistened with moisture. What an enterprise.

Both conspirators were up before light. They were toilers of the dark. Dark thoughts and dark deeds. It is amazing how even a dreadful scheme once hatched is all absorbing, and dedication unquestioned. This was no exception.

Donald and Jasper were at the door of *Empire Air Conditioning plc* before all the staff were installed. In their hands a shopping list that would bewilder the most experienced fitter.

'So, it's stainless steel you're after? Right. And these pieces and in these dimensions?' The assistant prodded at Donald's neatly compiled document. 'Right. And the rubber seals you have down here?' Further scrutiny of the list. A scratch of the head. 'You're absolutely sure?'

'Yes, yes. Just what we have written down.' Donald was impatient with the fool.

'What on earth are you building? Never filled out an order like this before. Could make Robocop from this lot.' The assistant's joke not far from the awful truth.

Inside Jasper's car the erratic jumble resembled a piece of sculpture on display at a modern art gallery. Somewhere amidst the lengths of stainless steel tubing and rubber seals Donald sat making devious plans.

'Get this home, and then we must find all we need to operate our glorious robot.' A voice from deep down beneath the metal pieces. 'The finest electronics and computer hardware we can assemble.'

At *Saturn Computer Supplies* Donald held out another list, and it too baffled the man at the desk.

'How much wire? You could make a clothes line from this lot.' He didn't wait for an answer and flitted down another aisle to bring back a tower of boxes. 'You going to install your own early warning system? Even the Government doesn't use this much storage? You sure about the size of this hard disk?' The man prattled on as he continued to collect items from high shelves and distant store rooms.

Finally he stood behind the mountain on his counter, hands on hips, proud he could supply all of Donald's requirements. No matter how ridiculous he regarded the items purchased.

'There! We have everything. Go to it Jasper. Build me the finest mechanical creature known to man.' Donald surveyed the mound of material now littering the living room floor.

'It will take time. Perfection cannot be rushed. Superior engineering and inventive design are not to be hurried.' Jasper was slurping on his words as he placed his tools down and pulled up his sleeves.

'Yes, yes. You can stop that nonsense. Just give

me my lethal robot.' Donald had no time for Jasper's chatter.

Night and day Jasper built, and night and day Donald fussed around and imagined the finished article in action.

First Jasper fixed multi-jointed limbs to the barrel-like body. Both of shimmering stainless steel. Arms with elbows and wrists. Legs with knees and ankles. Even lying there on the floor it was clear that this guy was going to be some athlete. On top of the rotund body Jasper attached a cylindrical head. Perfect symmetry.

'Excellent.' Donald rubbed his hands over the smooth shell. All going to plan.

Jasper slotted in the *organs* of the beast. State of the art computer hardware, supported by the most sophisticated software. Wiring proved the most tedious job. Jasper needed the hand of a surgeon and the eye of an owl. Threading any number of different coloured leads throughout the prostrate body.

'The life blood eh, Jasper?' Donald watched Jasper wrestle with the wiring. 'Arteries and veins, carrying the very essence of existence.' Uncomfortably ghoulish. Donald was just like Dr. Frankenstein watching his monster coming alive.

With only the power packs to insert, Jasper made sure that Donald was at his side. Moments like this don't come often. No old car batteries for this complex machine. Super slim, high capacity units snugly fitted into accommodating shelves.

'Everything in place.' Jasper's sunken eyes brightened. Maniac stare. He had worked day and night on this dastardly project, and he squinted through blackened lids and heavy bags.

'Let me have the pleasure.' Donald sucked back dribble.

'Here.' Jasper passed a flat-pad remote control panel. 'All physical movements programmed.'

'Let me see.' Donald examined the control. Fingers searching for the appropriate command. He found it.

The monstrous robot lifted itself from the floor. First one huge tubular leg, and then the other. Straightened a massive barrel body and rotated its head. Only a purr from the motors driving these parts. None of the ugly noises that showed Robert was active. Something eerie in that muffled murmur, that ghostly movement.

'Wow!' Donald watched it stretch to its full height. Not only was it built with the stockiness of a garbage truck, its head nearly reached the nine feet high ceiling of the living room. A colossal brute. Gleaming steel.

'What a handsome chap.' Jasper rolled his head in admiration.

'Excellent, Uncle. You have done well. Now, a name. With all this excitement we have not considered what we shall call *him*. Definitely male. How could a frighteningly gruesome robot that stands so threateningly above us be regarded as female?'

'You haven't met my cleaning lady,' Jasper added. He was in fear of that woman all right. A horrid witch who often had this supposedly fearful man shaking in his shoes.

'Maybe,' Donald dismissed. He wasn't really interested in such a digression. 'A name?' Donald touched the stainless steel. 'A name for my robot? And I don't want one of those prissy kids' names like Trevor or Robert. I need it to indicate the nature of the beast; his strength and his power, his dislike of weakness and failure, his determination to destroy those who have betrayed us.'

'So Rupert is out of the question?' Jasper was tired and didn't intend to be humorous. But he was.

'Fool! This robot is in the mould of a Roman or Viking god. Think! A name?' Donald was losing his cool.

'I have it.' Jasper's last chance according to Donald's expression. 'A name, ordinary to us all if spoken softly, yet everything you want in a name if shouted aloft, and proclaimed for all to admire.'

'Yes?'

'Victor!' Jasper spoke to emphasise the potential of the name.

'It was my granddad's middle name,' Donald retorted.

'Winner, champion, conqueror, defeating all. That's our Victor.' Jasper was selling it well.

'Victor. Hmm. Victor. Victor.' Donald sounded it out, louder and louder. Increasing the venom. 'Yes. It shall be Victor.' He turned to the brute of a robot as if he expected a response. 'Tonight, until morning, we will program Victor. And by tomorrow we may begin his training.'

'Okay,' Jasper responded with a groan. Another sleepless night.

Donald didn't feel the tiredness. Jasper's was evident from the descending bags cascading like mudslides below his eyes. But they were near completion as dawn arrived.

'Just one more thing.' Jasper puffed. 'I have allowed for voice variation. From fairy whisper to terrible bellow, is a fair description.'

'Good. I feel we shall be using more of those at the top of the terror scale.' Donald gleefully decided. 'So we are ready?'

'We are.'

A push of the button. Little change. Only the purr increased to a low whine.

'H...Hello, Victor.' Donald greeted his robot with a hint of hesitation.

'Honoured, Leader.' No misunderstanding. Precise language delivered in a mid-Atlantic accent. Even expensive software will provide only the one patronising dialect.

'Leader? Is that your doing, Jasper?'

'Thought it appropriate. Like it?' Jasper smirked.

'Not sure. Leader or Donald will do. They are synonymous, aren't they?' Self-satisfied grin from the ghastly boy.

'You do understand, Victor, that you must do as I say at all times.' Donald wanted to ensure the rules were laid down early.

'Already programmed, Leader.' Victor responded. Efficient mid-Atlantic reply, mid-range between pleasant and hostile.

'You have been built, created, Victor to perform certain tasks for me...and Jasper.' An afterthought. He'd deal with that problem later in the programme. 'But one definite job that you must complete without failure is the destruction of a traitor. One of your kind. Another robot.' Donald was insistent. 'You will receive more details later.'

Victor listened like a lamb. One huge gleaming mountain of pipework that almost filled the living room. His programming restricted independent thought and there was no questioning these duties. In fact, this lump of spanking new stainless steel tubing was quite a dummy. A witless idiot.

'Let me show you around.' Donald strolled through the door.

Victor lifted one thundering leg and thudded it down. With the one pace he was at the opening.

You know how some people are so keen on boating they decide to build their own craft. They buy the kit and carefully construct the hull in the garage; painstakingly attaching all the fittings. The day comes when, extremely excited, they prepare to take it to the water and launch their beloved boat. But NO! They didn't consider the dimensions. They can't get the thing out of the garage, and end up taking most of it apart to do so.

Well, it was somewhat similar with Victor being built in Donald's living room. Standing up he was nearly nine feet tall. The doorway seven feet at the most. Crassshhhh!

Victor's head and shoulders removed an enormous chunk of masonry and plaster. A slab that was violently despatched, that thundered down very nearly crushing Jasper's skull.

Unfortunately Donald was well up the front garden path when Victor struck the inner wall. Frenzied waving failed to prevent further demolition. With a second stride Victor had removed a similar sized piece of brickwork above the front door. This time Jasper was wise enough to stand well clear.

Victor was oblivious to the damage. Unable to realise he was covered in debris and dust, or understand the scratches that now scarred his brand new dazzling suit.

'Damn!' Donald stamped up and down like a child refused an ice cream. The tantrum of a very weird boy indeed.

Chapter Fourteen

'What on earth!' Mr. Dobbins was blown out of a not unpleasant dream by a loud banging. He hunted for the clock. It toppled and spilled to the floor, where he continued to grapple with it. 'Six-thirty!' His knees were still on the bed but his forehead was on the carpet. He could easily fall asleep again where he was. The rhythm was returning, and so was the dream.

Bang! Bang! Bang!

Somebody was impatient and determined to wake the dead.

Bang! Bang! Bang!

'Okay, okay.' Mr. Dobbins slid down the carpeted stairs. His back to the wall. He was holding on to his dream.

Bang! Bang! Bang!

'All right, what the...' Mr. Dobbins' voice trailed off as he pulled the front door open.

Amassed in the porch were four policemen, and more officers lined the path.

'Mr. William Dobbins?' Sergeant Billet's face was severe and puffed.

'Of course.' Bill Dobbins was fazed.

'We have a warrant to search this property.' Billet flashed a piece of paper in front of Bill Dobbins' eyes and pushed past into the hallway. Several men followed. 'And we will need to interview you and your son.'

'What's going on?' Mr. Dobbins managed to squeak once his head was on straight.

'We'll get to that in a moment. First we need to locate your robot. Where is he?'

'Robert? He's in the basement.' Mr. Dobbins indicated by pointing at the door.

'What's going on?' Michael and his mother were at the top of the stairs, bleary-eyed and screwed-up faces.

'Nothing to worry about dear.' Mr. Dobbins assured her. 'Must be some mistake. I'll sort it out.'

At that moment three constables clambered up the basement steps carrying the prone body of Robert.

'Robert!' Michael stumbled down the staircase. 'Leave my robot alone. You can't take Robert away.' He pulled at the sleeves of the policemen.

'Take it easy, son. Serious investigation taking place here.' Billet was in real police officer mode. 'Into the front room. I'll talk to them in there. You continue with the rest of the house. You know what we're looking for.' Billet's voice trailed to a whisper as he instructed one of the officers.

Robert was laid on the floor. Michael and his father sat on the sofa. Billet stalked the room. Mrs. Dobbins made tea.

'What is all this?' Mr. Dobbins was annoyed and confused. Far too early for him to get to grips with anything complicated.

'I have to tell you,' Billet started, 'this is a very serious matter. A security van has been robbed less than a mile from here.'

'So? What's that got to do with us?' Bill Dobbins was waking up.

'Plenty, I'm afraid. Witnesses report that the thief who viciously stole several thousands of pounds was a metallic person. Steel from head to foot. None other than a robot. Yes a robot.' Billet turned to look directly at the slumped body of Robert, motionless on the floor. A body waiting for burial. 'This fellow is the only robot around here. And, this boy,' Billet turned to Michael, 'is the only person who owns one. Do I make myself clear?'

Michael and his father exchanged confused glances. Robert had been inactive in the basement for days. If he had been in trouble someone would have had to break in, steal Robert, somehow convince him to comply, bring him back after the crime and leave the house without anyone knowing. Other than that, one of the people in the house would have to be involved. They weren't. In no way was it Michael's mother, and to think that Gran was out robbing security vans was, at the best, hilarious.

'Well?' Sergeant Billet enquired. 'What have you got to say?'

'Robert hasn't been anywhere. Neither have we. It couldn't have been Robert who did this.' Michael was emphatic.

'So you are denying any involvement in this crime. And you expect us to believe that if your robot was not the offender, that there is another bleeding robot out there causing havoc on my patch?' Billet shook his head in disbelief. 'You taking me for a mug or what?'

'I can vouch for my son and...Robert.' Mr. Dobbins stood up to show his defiance.

'I see.' Billet mused. 'I see. Well we have witnesses as I told you. One of whom is in the patrol car outside. If you wait here we'll see if he's able to recognise the culprit. Soon put an end to this nonsense. Only making it harder for yourselves.' A confident smile by the exiting policeman.

Billet returned with a dazed security guard. An awkwardly uniformed guy in his twenties. *Templeton Securities* emblazoned in silver on his dark blue tunic.

'You okay Steven?' Billet asked the young man. 'He's still a bit shocked after the incident.' Billet tried to explain to Michael and his dad.

'I'm fine. Just shook me a bit. Never seen nothing like that before,' Steven muttered.

'Now I want you to take a look at something. And don't be concerned, the power's off.' Billet pulled gently at Steven's elbow.

'What? Power off? He's not around here is he?' Steven began shaking from the shoulders down.

'Easy, son. Important we get this identification. You're safe as houses here. Now if you'd move aside and let Steven have a butchers.' Billet waved Michael and Mr. Dobbins away from the prostrate robot.

'There, Steven.' Billet beamed. 'What do you see?'

Steven's eyes widened and he pulled the fringe of his hair to one side. Took a step forward and bent down. 'I see a load of junk lying on the floor. Rusty bucket, old dustbin and what looks like the contents of my dad's shed.'

'You don't see the robot that attacked you and stole the money?' Billet was gobsmacked.

'Robot? That ain't no robot. That's a pile of scrap metal.' Steven started to chuckle. He was recovering.

'So if that isn't the robot that committed this crime,' Billet began, 'what exactly are we looking for?'

'This bleeder was a monster. Twice my height and in bright, shining metal. Not a heap of bits and pieces like this jumble of tin waste.' Steven didn't like remembering his assailant.

Michael and his father exchanged glances. Another robot? That would be incredible.

'Your son not been up to his tricks again, and built another flipping robot has he?' Sergeant Billet asked, desperate to solve this mystery.

'No.' Michael answered the question for his father.

Sergeant Billet gathered all his mob together and ushered them out of the house. There was no doubting this was a time for a cuppa. He could smell the station brew from there.

'Who else could built a robot?' Mr. Dobbins asked Michael once the Bobbies had left.

Michael scratched his head. 'No idea. Sounds a sophisticated one. Perhaps some electronics firm has been experimenting. But, why would they get it to rob a security van?'

'Who would build a robot and use it for evil purposes?' Mr. Dobbins was thinking aloud.

The penny suddenly dropped. Michael had one person in mind. He kept quiet. Time to do some detective work. Robot building would get a bad name if something wasn't done about this outrage.

Chapter Fifteen

Donald Clipper sat on the floor of the living room. There was a beam of satisfaction on his face. At his feet a mound of money, neatly packaged. Uncle Jasper stood beside the loot, slobbering over the notes. 'Success, my boy. Victor by name and victor by action.'

'I feel good about the future here, Jasper. I have planned well. Is Victor in his hideaway?' Donald rubbed his hands.

'Yes, my boy. Victor is in the truck. A splendid vehicle I bought from the furniture store. Still has the company name on the sides. No one will ever know what lies within. A fuming fiend.'

'He was so good this morning. Did you see the faces of those security twits? Scared out of their trousers. Awesome.' Donald tittered.

'How much did we get?' Jasper smacked his lips.

'Twelve thousand quid!' Donald sniggered. 'Victor stole for us, twelve thousand beautiful pounds.' Donald picked up some bundles and tossed them in the air. 'What fun.'

'Are we ready for that tin head, Robert?' Jasper asked.

'One more test, I think, before we destroy that viper.' Donald decided. 'We must be vigilant. He is a snake, and we must ensure that Victor is in prime form for the task.' Donald let out a low chuckle.

'What will be Victor's next venture?' Jasper ground his teeth.

'The school. Victor will go to Granford Manor School and scare the living daylights out of all those snivelling kids. I know they despise me. Never liked me. Treated me worse than dirt. But, I'll get them back. Oh, yes, I will show them what Donald Clipper can do.' Donald was freaking out.

'The school.' Jasper was repeating like some simpleton. 'The school, hmm, Victor would be a frightening visitor there.'

'Get the truck parked just down the road from the school entrance. When I tell you let Victor approach the playground. I will take over from there. My remote control will assist me in dealing with my school chums. Yes indeed.'

Playgrounds are playgrounds. Frantic activity and a cauldron of noise. Football games criss-crossing each other. Girls running around screaming at nothing. Scrums of plotters in serious consultation. A cut knee. Hurt feelings. The listener, a bulky woman with a whistle.

With that din you don't hear a giant robot

approaching. In the intensity of the game you don't look to see the monstrous shadow spread across your playground. But, there is always one observer. One child left out. Not selected for the football team, not included in the corner gossip, no need to scream, not hurt or looking for comfort. Even then it takes a few seconds for your brain to believe it and for your jaw to stop juddering.

'My God!' From the edge of the playground tarmac a small girl counting beads managed the cry. 'Oh, no!'

Two or three children first heard the shriek and added their cries of horror. Then the infection spread. A playground of friendly chaos extinguished to silence. Gaping mouths and bulging eyes.

'One of yours Dobbins?' a shivering boy asked Michael. If you're the only robot builder you can expect such questions.

Michael's mouth could have caught an eagle. 'It's not mine. It's a beauty though.'

Victor had stopped at the gates. The woman with the whistle had it to her mouth, but was frozen with fear.

Donald, hiding behind a car, examined his remote control. An advanced device that allowed him to command Victor through a digital microphone.

Victor moved forward. Massive legs that would crush a child. With each step children fled from the crashing limbs. An arm was lowered. Neatly arranged fingers delicately picked up each football that still rolled with the wind in the space evacuated by the frightened children. Victor's pulverising fist reduced the plastic and rubber balls to lumps of used gum.

Other toys and cherished belongings were snatched, or their owners forced to drop. These too followed the fate of the balls. Compressed or distorted beyond recognition by the mechanical bully, so evilly controlled by Donald Clipper.

Quentin Marigold had by this time been alerted. Unlike his predecessor he wasn't a man for confrontation, and like most of the staff of Granford Manor School, had found a desk to hide under. From his refuge he couldn't reach the phone, but he'd done the next bravest thing; he'd ordered Mrs. Praddle, the school secretary, to phone the police.

Victor was finished with the spoils from the playground. Or, rather, Donald had made sure no article of enjoyment was left in one piece, and that every kid was saying his prayers. Although from his position he couldn't see, he trusted that Michael Dobbins in particular was wetting himself. *Now, this is a robot for you, Michael. You can forget that mongrel tin pot that you built. Scruffy, dilapidated load of scrap metal. This is a real robot. This one means business.*

Victor's attention now centred on the school

building. At his height he could reach both storeys of the main block. All was in Donald's grasp. Where to start?

'Oi!' A figure was standing next to Victor's left leg. 'I'm talking to you.' A hero had emerged. Children quaking in the playground. Staff in their shelters. One man had shrugged off his fear and was standing up to this metal invader. Leonard Climp, sports master, wasn't going to let some mechanical monstrosity boss around the hardman of Granford Manor.

Victor turned to identify the intruder. Donald received a close-up of Climp's face on his control panel screen. You know, just like those close-ups you get from the back of a dessert spoon. All distorted so the image is cartoon in appearance. Climp was puffed at the cheeks and sporting a huge bulbous nose. Hawk eyes that bulged and a moustache like a beaver.

'You, whatever you are, we aren't impressed with this anti-social behaviour.' Climp craned his neck and jabbed a finger.

Climp's lips were plastic and glazed. And between the inflated mouth his yellow teeth were tusks gnashing away.

Donald acted.

Victor lifted the sports master off his feet and marched him onto the playing field. Some of the children turned to watch his progress. With each step the squelching grass gave up water to the robot's heavy tread.

At the far end of the field rugby posts still stood. In summer you only needed to remove one set to mark the track. Bates, the school groundsman knew that. Victor lifted Leonard Climp and twisted his atrociously patterned sweater around one of the uprights and left him struggling high above the grass. It was at these same posts that Climp had harangued Donald Clipper for his *poor tackling and gutless performance* in the house rugby. Now Donald smiled smugly into the control panel screen. *Serves him right!*

Billet wasn't hurrying to send out a squad car. Yes, it was an emergency. Bleeding robot again. Kids in danger at the school. But he knew what he'd find. Knew he could do nothing. And, worst of all knew that the law could not be upheld. It was taking all the fun out of being a ruddy policeman.

'Harry, you and Pete head over to Granford Manor School. Incident. Keep me informed.' Sergeant Billet wouldn't give full details. He knew this pair had had it up to their helmets with flipping robots.

In his office, Quentin Marigold cowered under his desk. *Such a beast. A huge metallic machine laying siege to the school. What action was necessary? As captain of the ship he needed to make that decision.*

Staying put and keeping out of sight and saving his own butt was the answer.

Victor left Leonard Climp groaning from his high perch. Like a sailor in the crow's nest of a ship. Victor headed for the main academic block and the school's administration area. Donald had a goal. Inside there were some atrocious examination results that he wasn't so proud of, and a condemning report that might bring his parents back from exile in South Africa. He was having too much fun to be smothered by them.

Victor's tubular arms popped open the window of Quentin Marigold's office, and with his extensive reach began dragging out the tall, green filing cabinet that held precious school documents. From under his desk Quentin watched the progress of the cabinet. Knew the value contained in each drawer. Couldn't let such crucial paperwork leave the school. Quentin acted out of panic and duty. He jumped out of his lair and leaped up, onto the piece of furniture that was just about to disappear out of the first floor window.

Donald saw the headmaster riding the filing cabinet as if it were a rodeo steer. As Victor swung it round Quentin Marigold held on for dear life. Thank heavens for drawer handles. Out of the school grounds strode the gleaming robot. Children in the playground, still paralysed with fright, watched their headmaster clutching on to his precious records. Dangling legs swaying wildly with every long step of the robot's progress.

Victor was in the truck within seconds of leaving the school gate. Quentin Marigold had lost his grip when the robot entered the rear of the vehicle, and was left sprawled in the road, flapping an arm and moaning. Jasper secured the back doors and drove off.

'Mind that lorry, Pete,' Harry warned as they approached the school entrance. 'You'll have us in hospital, you will.'

There was only the aftermath of Victor's visit to survey when Harry Evans and Pete drove into the school grounds. The fat lady with the whistle was counselling a group of young children, whilst the remainder of the playground were swapping stories. Michael was at the centre of a large group. A huddle firing questions at him about the magnificent robot that had just rampaged through their school. Leonard Climp had slid down the rugby posts as far as the cross bar and was balanced at the stomach, so that he rocked gently. Quentin Marigold was being dusted down by Mrs. Praddle, and being told what a brave man he was.

'Where do we start, Harry?' Pete scratched his head and questioned his superior.

'Another bleeding robot mess. Billet knew about this. Didn't bother to warn us.' Harry was not amused. He wanted to jump up and down on his hat and scream, but he was a police officer and there was a situation to deal with. How he wished he'd been a sewage engineer instead.

Chapter Sixteen

'You should have seen it, Dad.' Michael spluttered in his father's face. 'It was enormous. Made Robert look puny. And glistening steel, or what? It was awesome. Wow! What a robot.'

'Ease up. Where did you see it?' Mr. Dobbins pushed Michael's shoulders down so that he sat. 'Give it to me slowly.'

'At school.' Michael caught his breath. 'It came into the playground. A monster. Could have been ten or twelve feet tall. Scared the living daylights out of everyone. Smashed all the kids' stuff. Took *Climpy* out to the field and fixed him to the rugby posts. Then stole a cabinet out of the head's office. Should have seen *Old Rubber Gloves*. He climbed onto it and came out of the window riding it, as this titan dragged it out. Cor, wish I'd made that brute.'

'No you don't. We've had enough trouble with your own invention without getting the blame for this fiasco.' Michael's dad had a long memory. 'Why did this robot come to the school? Were the police called?'

'They were there all right. As baffled as everyone. But, you'd have loved this beauty, Dad. It was wicked.'

'Great job.' Donald tapped the filing cabinet. 'Worked like a dream. You missed some wonderful moments this afternoon, Jasper.'

'Smooth operation, boy. Split-second timing and accurate planning. If I do say so.' Jasper congratulated himself.

'There. Gone! All my bad grades and stinking reports. Clean as a whistle now.' Donald tore up the records with glee. 'Might as well do the rest.' He found the files of the school swats and with the same enthusiasm destroyed those. 'Jasper, start a fire in the garden, there's lots of fuel.' It gave Donald great pleasure to find the beige *Dobbins M.* file and rip it into ever increasing shreds. Showering the front room with confetti.

Back at the station Sergeant Billet was storming around spilling his beloved tea as he thundered from office to office. 'Let me have it once again PC Evans.' Billet always referred to officers in that way when he was peeved.

'Well,' Harry began, 'seems that our rogue robot has been on the rampage again. At the school he picked on the kids in the playground, some have-a-go teacher who was left fixed to the rugby posts and nicked a piece of furniture from the headmaster's office.'

'Get it written up.' Billet knew it was a waste of time, but rules were rules. 'Full report.'

'Right,' Harry groaned.

'Any sign of our man? That robot leave a trail? Bleeding great contraption made of polished metal can't flipping disappear without trace, can it? Are we supposed to be policemen or what? Blooming CID are useless. Call themselves detectives. It's a joke.'

'Thin air, Sarge. Vanished. No blooming sign of the contraption.' Harry Evans thundered off up the corridor to begin typing.

'Everything is going to plan. This is the most fun I've had for ages.' Donald rocked on the spot. 'Money and notoriety, even though we can't take the credit just yet. But, I'm sure there'll come a time when the world will know of this.' Donald was getting carried away, clucking with laughter.

'Excellent, my boy.' Jasper bustled by, hissing through his teeth.

'It's time for repayment. Time to rid this town of that ridiculous tinpot reject that has the cheek to call itself a robot. Robert must be reduced to the only thing fitting. A pile of redundant metal. A rust heap of rubbish. Because, that is all he is.' Donald's bitterness was still evident with the snarling of his curled lips.

'You have a plan, nephew?' Jasper enquired.

'Not just a plan, a master plan! A finely tuned strategy that will finish that scum robot for ever.' Donald hailed Jasper to his side.

'Tell me all.' Jasper slobbered expectantly.

'Look here.' Donald held an embossed card for Jasper to study. 'An invitation to a party. For that idiot Michael and his stupid load of junk. At the adventure park. Every kind of activity and delight. Every opportunity to annihilate the traitor, Robert. Horrifically smashed in a dreadful collision. Disintegration into parcels of waste metal at his maker's feet. I can feel the excitement now. And the satisfaction. It will be a wondrous day.'

'Invitation?' Jasper needed it spelled out.

'Yes, we invite lots of kids, and especially that dumbo Dobbins. An extravagant celebration with all the rides free. We get him there with Robert and set up the most murderous end to that dimwit's existence. With a surprise guest of course. Victor arrives to dismember the goon. Do you get it?' Donald ground his hands together and gurgled his pleasure.

The school playground was buzzing with inquisitive chatter. Most of the elaborate invitations had arrived before the children had left for school, and they were being brandished around the huddles of pupils before registration bell.

'Whose party is it?' Michael quizzed his friends.

'Secret, apparently. Who cares? Freebie at Willington Wild Adventure Park, don't get that often.' An excited voice explained. 'You should see some of those rides. Boy next door went on the big one. Call it the *Kamikaze Tsunami*. Massive drop and a ton of water. He nearly messed his pants.' Sniggers all round.

'Yeah, but it's unusual to get one for Robert as well,' Michael puzzled.

'One of the lads now, your robot. Be a hoot if he's there as well.'

Michael was a little dubious. He couldn't fully trust the tin man to stay out of trouble. And certainly didn't want to be embarrassed in front of his mates.

Everybody was going. No one was prepared to turn this one down. Only natural for a load of kids to relish the thought of free funfair rides and the promise of a feast. Didn't matter who was funding it or whose birthday was being celebrated.

'Best behaviour. No trouble. Keep with me and don't wander.' Michael briefed Robert. 'All these kids are my friends. If you let me down I'll take out your batteries and fling them in the lake. You can say goodbye to freedom. You'll stay in the basement as an ornament. Like a stuffed animal. Stuck there immobile. Got it?' Michael was serious.

'Robert understands. You can rely on Robert.' A confident confirmation.

When Michael and Robert arrived at the entrance to Willington Wild Adventure Park a small group had assembled and others were being dropped off by ferrying parents. Mothers making final adjustments to their little darlings' clothes. For kids they were smartly dressed, and all clutched their elaborate invitations that Donald had devised. It wasn't the din of school break time. A lower noise. No yelling. Merely the buzz of excitement and expectation. All eyes on the arriving vehicles. Greeting a new and tidier version of the kid they knew from the playground.

'Gather round.' A portly middle-aged man waved his arms to collect everyone together. 'Let's get you through here and on to some fantastic rides. The Park's relatively empty and should stay that way for the next three hours.' Jolly old bloke who was used to ushering kids about. He snatched at the invites. Plucking them from flapping hands as the mass of children struggled through the entrance turnstiles.

'All to ourselves. Wow!' A chirpy voice announced with glee.

'Whose party is this?' another enquired. 'Anybody know?' A running boy blurted. An enquiry without real enthusiasm. Too much temptation ahead.

'Some sort of surprise. That's what they're saying. Generous, eh?' Running parallel an equally spirited boy added.

Donald and Jasper watched the invasion. Tinted windows on the truck hid their identity and their cruel searching eyes. In the back Victor stood, battery packs on charge.

'There he is!' Donald spied Robert clomping along beside Michael and a group of friends. 'Everything to plan.' He bared his teeth and sniggered.

'*Haunted Cavern*. Okay with you Robert?' Michael tugged as his robot's arm.

'Whatever you decide, Master.' Robert clonked along faster to keep up with the crowd. He was as eager as the next. Absorbing the atmosphere of excitement. Though he wasn't really sure what all the fuss was about.

'You ride with me. Boy, is this scary.' Michael helped Robert into the carriage and secured his safety bar. Boys and girls clambered in behind, filling up all the rows. No one had seen a robot experience an adventure park ride, and now this one was riding up front to face one of the most fearful courses they weren't going to miss it.

At the first curve a plastic skeleton swooped to graze the occupants, accompanied by a wailing and wild cackling from three nearby witches reeling about their cauldron. Everybody screamed as their heads were dragged sideways by the turning car. Except, of course, Robert, who sat rigid and unmoved. Incapable of comprehending the behaviour of those around him.

Coffin lids lifted, evil goblins spat venomously at the shrieking children, spider-webs hung low and dusty, headless Elizabethans ghosted past, smoke and mists, groans and clattering chains and all manner of spectres chilled the spines of the ducking children. Only Robert stayed upright against the macabre onslaught. Only Robert picked up all the debris from that gruesome journey. A bold figurehead collecting the litter of demons. Amidst the pasty-faced children was the most extraordinary figure. Draped in every feasible material and vegetable dye that was thrown from the collection of despicable figures that inhabited the *Haunted Cavern*.

'Phew, that was scary,' Michael puffed as he tipped out of the carriage. Stretching his eyes with relief.

Grunts of agreement from the rest of the kids who were straightening their clothes and shrugging off their fear.

'Scary?' Robert looked up the meaning. 'Pleasant car ride with the lights out. Many people to greet us in the tunnel.' Robert's metallic voice decided.

'Robert! Look at yourself,' Michael cried. 'What a mess.'

Heads turned and from initial giggles there developed a mighty roar. Robert was almost an exhibit himself.

'You look like Frankenstein's bride.' Michael nearly choked on his own joke.

But he did. Robert looked just like that. Fake blood ran from his head and down his dustbin body. Green goo hung from his forehead. White gauze tumbled from his bucket head like flowing ectoplasm and trailed behind, occasionally being flicked and floated by the channelled breeze.

Michael couldn't let Robert look a fool or a ghoul for long and cleaned off the offending material.

'Where next?' Michael asked.

'Let's go steady for this one, Mrs. Frankenstein might want to get her head straightened in preparation for the *Pirate Boat*,' a giggling boy suggested.

'Yeah. *Teacups* it is,' a girl concluded. A prissy attraction, but just the one ride would be acceptable, the gang agreed.

'No problem here, Robert.' Michael settled him in with four other passengers. 'Cars swing a bit as we go round, but nothing frightening.'

'Fine,' Robert acknowledged with an annoying tinny echo.

Slowly each wagon creaked into action and began its circuit. Cars rocked and slid a little. Quite tame. Gradually each unit spun, shuffling the occupants to one end of the seat. Michael felt the full force of Robert's rough steel body.

'If we hold this lever to brake the car, and then let go we will get a greater swing,' Michael informed the whole group, but no one in particular.

Robert grabbed it, before any lily-white child's hand could have the fun.

These are basically fairground attractions and the mechanics made for mere mortals; kids and know-all fathers. Certainly not robots without any idea of the torque they can exert.

Blue smoke filled the air as the pretty teacup was halted with an ear-deafening screech. Fortune kept the children seated. Their backs forced against the rear of the seat.

'Let it go!' Michael screamed at Robert.

An obedient robot always obeys his master. Robert did just that.

Bounding into the air. Almost leap-frogging the next car, the pretty teacup lurched forward. Tiny hands clutched at the restraining bar as their carriage took flight. Anchor bolts sheared with a steely twang and the teacup vaulted the next. Occupants' mouths agape. A quick flight. The cup landing amidst sparks and scraping metal. Settling with the plop of a returning space capsule. Stunned children thanking their lucky stars.

'Not exactly to plan.' Michael managed to tell his robot. 'Help these guys out, can you?' Displeasure in his tone.

'That was fantastic, Robert.'

'Yeah, best trip I've had.'

'You're the man, Robert.'

'Where next?'

Adulation all round. Except from the boy who knew better. Michael would have to play along. Only he knew the danger they all faced at the hands of his idiot robot.

'Food's up!' A moon-faced girl announced.

'Last one there's a dummy!'

Frantic athletics as the gang of kids headed for the Park Café. Each group heeding the call had homed in on the refreshments. There were tributaries of sprinting children meeting along the main track to the food. A buffalo stampede. Waddling toddlers had to be snatched from the path of the charging animals by their vigilant mothers.

Robert strode sedately. No urgency. He would have to watch the rest gorge themselves on hotdogs and coke. It wasn't the same fun being a robot who didn't eat.

Michael sat Robert down near the napkins and condiments, while he joined in the bun fight. The tubby man returned to ensure everyone was fed, and to prevent disputes being settled with a volley of burger buns used as battling Frisbees.

'Now to the *Pirate Boat*!' A boy with a mustard mouth and barbecue sauce cheek declared.

The journey was slower. Fries have that effect. Doesn't do to rush things when greasy chips are lying heavy in your gut.

'Get in the back.' Michael ordered Robert. 'You go higher and get a great ride in that position.'

'If you say so, Master.' Robert duly obliged and sat at the tip of the bow.

'No nonsense this time. Just because some of the kids think you are great don't let it go to your stupid tin head. Got it?' Michael whispered fiercely as he plonked down beside Robert.

Full with bubbly kids the giant pendulum was set in motion, accompanied by skull and crossbones music and a Long John Silver look-alike who prattled on forever with *shiver me timbers* and *look lively me hearties*, and other senseless pirate cliches.

Gradually the faltering movement increased to a rhythm that lifted the *crew* off their seats, and prompted the fragile passengers to give off distress signals. By the time the *Pirate Boat* ride was at full speed distress had become frantic shrieking, and fragile was now scared brainless.

'This is so cool.' Michael spluttered as he looked down vertically on the passengers at the stern. 'What a blast! We're right overhead.'

Michael hadn't seen Robert smuggle away two souvenirs from the food break. They had fascinated the robot, so much so that he had walked off with them. Two large plastic tomatoes that were full of the stickiest tomato ketchup. You know the type. They usually sit in the middle of the table at some greasy restaurant. Tacky containers advertising their contents.

Michael was loving this ride. Too engrossed in having a spectacular time to keep Robert out of more trouble. He was oblivious to the robot's next trick.

As the *Pirate Boat* reached the apex of its next swing Robert decided to give the bottles a squeeze. The grip of a robot clutching a frail sauce dispenser can empty that container in an instant. Gravity, a great assistant, can direct that fluid directly downwards. Not a perfect science. There needs to be an allowance for wind direction, and perfect timing. But this was no real experiment.

A stream of red syrup plummeted. And amidst the excitement came terror. Screaming mouths were abruptly stifled, and filled with the falling ketchup. Stray flying droplets, breeze assisted, splattered faces and clothing throughout the last seat of passengers and neighbouring rows. And when the boat swung again, leaving the victims at the top, tomato spit and released and shaken globes of red liquid rained down on Michael and his friends at their end. Even Robert was splashed by his own returning gluey ketchup.

With every swing the tomato ketchup was sent backwards and forwards. An even distribution not always in its pure form. Dribbling and dripping on every groaning passenger.

Slowing down there was chaos as everyone scraped off or spat out the gooey sauce. Angry eyes searching for the offender.

'Was that you?' Michael pulled at Robert's paint-tin arm and pushed his face, freckled with ketchup, against Robert's head and microphone ear.

'Me? What?' Robert innocently asked.

'Covered us all in tomato sauce?' Michael continued.

'Of course. Did you enjoy it?' Robert straightened himself. Proud of his actions.

'You idiot! How dare you ruin my day? Why on earth did you do it?'

'Robert wanted to make people happy.' Sadness in his slow iron voice.

The ride had stopped now and Michael pushed Robert into a corner away from the spattered kids. 'Happy?' Michael pulled at Robert's arm. 'How can making us a mess with this sticky stuff make us flipping happy?'

Robert opened his hands and released the crumpled dispensers. He twisted one round and displayed the label. ***Crompton's Ketchup - Squeeze it tight for a child's delight.*** 'Surely Robert delighted you, Master?'

'You fool! It doesn't mean you're supposed to shower us with it. It goes on food, not on faces, shirts, hair...' Michael stamped his feet. 'What am I going to do with you. You are such a pest. Such a...load of trouble.'

'Come on Michael, we're going on the roller coaster.' A small girl with a huge smile tugged at Michael's sleeve. 'Bring Robert, he's fun.'

'Last ride, Robert. Do you hear me? I can't stand the strain any longer. They're going to lynch me when they realise who coated them with Crompton's Ketchup. After this we are going. Got it?' Michael followed in the footsteps of the skipping girl, still fuming.

Robert was a little confused. He plodded along behind, upset that his master was again angry with him.

'They're heading for the roller coaster, Jasper. Get Victor ready. It's our chance.' Donald Clipper gnashed his teeth. 'The party's over, Robert.'

'All is in hand. A daring plan that will seal the fate of that clutter of pots.' Jasper sucked back the saliva that threatened to spill from his mouth onto the papers he nursed in his lap.

It was quite a ride, the roller coaster. Willington's called it the *Dragon's Lair*, as there was a part of the circuit where the wagons went through a fibreglass cave inhabited by a plastic green dragon that rotated its head and breathed flame. Well, some flimsy material lit in red that flapped about to look like fire. There was also a large loop that took screaming passengers upside down at speed, and photographed you looking plain stupid.

It was a quiet time for the Park and the long queue of the weekend was down to a trickle. Michael and Robert were encouraged to take a front seat in the wagon. Having a robot well positioned in the photo would be a bonus. Michael didn't argue, he loved the thrill of being the 'driver'.

Only a few people saw Uncle Jasper guide the huge robot down the service road that led to the start of *Dragon's Lair*. No need for panic. It was obviously a new exhibit that was being trundled into position. So many strange attractions that it barely invited a second look. Victor followed obediently behind the crouched figure of Jasper as he ducked and dived towards the stretch of track he needed.

Donald waited in the truck. Director of operations. He would bide his time before he received the adulation of the crowd.

On the ride everyone was seated and buckled in. In the supervisor's kiosk they were ready to start.

On a lower section of the rails, out of sight, Jasper worked. Despite his unpleasant appearance and hideous plans, Jasper was a skilful engineer. The click of a switch, and at each heel and at both wrists he provided Victor with a set of four glistening steel wheels. Wheels that clamped onto the outside of the rail exactly. Jasper pushed and pulled at the robot to ensure free running. Victor was set.

At a pedestrian pace the snaking cars began their journey. Grinding along the track. Jabbering kids shuffling in their seats. Michael and Robert at the front. They were leaders on an enthralling expedition.

At a similar pace, but with deadly intent, Victor was set in motion. Travelling in the opposite direction. A lethal ambush.

Michael's hair blew straight at the first drop. An increase in speed. And an increase in the sounds of delight from the passengers. Michael's body shuddered at a gentle corner. He held on tight. Robert looked blankly ahead. Camera eyes picking out the undulations in the railway. His computer calculated velocity, angle of descent and other unwarranted data. This he ignored with the invigoration of the ride.

Victor's motor took him up the gentle incline

towards the base of the large loop. To a point where the roller coaster car would be travelling at its maximum speed. Where he could lie in wait.

Like a bobsleigh on the Cresta Run the leading car shook and clattered. Up and down the hummocky track and in and out of the *Dragon's Lair*.

Michael tugged at Robert's arm as they entered the base of the loop. Silence spread like suffocating treacle. All passengers held their breath.

Until...at the summit...the car plunged. And with that descent came the ear-piercing yells that were a mixture of thrills and fears. High-pitched exclamations of tribal emotions.

Victor heard them above him. Donald Clipper heard them from his hideaway, through his speaker. Jasper, partially hidden by a tree, watched and waited, an idiot grin on his face.

Victor's brakes were set. Solid and menacing he loomed over the rails. The oncoming carriage would meet immovable resistance at high speed. Robert would be destroyed. Donald Clipper, full of vengeance, had not considered the fate of all the children who accompanied him.

'Oh no!' Michael was the first to see Victor. First to understand the disaster ahead.

Robert was alerted. The screams behind him died away as in turn the children saw the stainless steel hulk lying in wait. Their faces fixed in horror. Robert's hard disk worked promptly to analyse the situation. Split seconds. No escape suggested.

There was no stopping the impact. It was inevitable. A colossal metal robot was directly in their path. They ducked down in a desperate move to avoid destruction.

The car whistled past without touching Victor. As if he were invisible, a hologram. Only the flash of his gleaming steel and the hiss of air. No crash at all.

With a creak and some grating noises the car came to a halt. An attendant rushed to help. Slowly heads bobbed to the surface. Very shaken.

'We missed it.' Michael croaked. 'How did that happen?'

Robert was ready to explain. 'That ugly robot that was fixed to the track,' Robert began, 'occupied the outer portion of the rail. His wheels were clamped on the exterior. Whereas the vehicle that carried us, for safety reasons, has the wheels fitted inside. We missed colliding with that *thing* because we were able to slip inside his ridiculous legs.' Robert was taking this personally. Michael had never seen him so agitated.

Jasper had covered his eyes as he saw the car about to thunder into Victor. Donald only saw the image of Robert about to be obliterated. When both scrambled eagerly to study the aftermath they saw nothing. Where was the mutilated car, the pieces of tin from the Judas robot? A collision should surely have produced a scene of utter devastation. But there was nothing.

'Jasper! What happened? Where are the crushed remnants of that tin-head robot?' Donald screamed down the intercom.

'I'm not sure. Victor is still there. Stuck firm to the track. But the car...the robot...are gone. Escape was impossible. As if they flew right through him.' Jasper was mystified.

'Follow that lump of junk. Set Victor after him. He will not evade us again.'

Jasper released the wheel clamps. Victor stretched upright, unaware of his failure. A colossus.

'Find that traitor, Robert, and destroy him. Do you understand, Victor?' Donald stabbed at his remote control.

'Victor understands.' A rumble of a voice. Nothing like the metallic syllables of Michael's robot.

Michael dragged himself from the car, legs still wobbly. 'Let's get a coke. That was some ride.'

Every head nodded agreement. The huddle moved at a crawl towards the drink kiosk.

'You kids watch out!' An attendant shouted from behind. 'That ruddy monster is heading this way.'

Michael looked over his shoulder. Looming above the shouting man and his office was Victor. A giant head and winged shoulders. A titanic bust. Almost godlike against the smoke-grey sky.

'Run!' Michael shouted. 'Get the hell out of here.'

Michael grabbed Robert's arm and pulled him along. Up a paved pathway between bushes and trees. An entrance of sorts. Some cover. Out of sight. The group had split like a fire-burst. All directions. Michael and Robert were on their own.

'Why did he try that?' Michael thought aloud. 'What's his game? Could have killed us. Well me, at least. And smashed you to bits.' Michael corrected himself.

'It's a robot thing. My business.' Robert spoke slower and apparently seriously. 'Let Robert deal with this. Must not hurt you, Master.' Icy metallic tone.

'No, Robert. It's for both of us to face. We can do it.'

The undergrowth exploded in their faces. Victor's leading leg crashed through. They watched their startled faces appear as a reflection on the intruding limb.

'In here.' Michael yanked Robert's hand and led him into a cabin. A log boat bobbed on a small reservoir of water. 'Must be a ride.' Michael looked at the sign swinging above his head.

Kamikaze Tsunami

'Oh...cr...crikey!' Michael stammered.

Nine feet tall glistening steel robots aren't easy to camouflage. Especially emitting frenzied roars at Donald's direction. And now Victor was thumping around the adventure park like a marauding ogre he had a vast audience. Most of which were certain this was a stunt staged by the management. And what a stunt! The robot was crushing small buildings and knocking aside trees and bushes. Real theatre. A crowd had gathered by the main reception, around the large pool area where the log boats from *Kamikaze Tsunami* finished the course with an enormous explosion of water.

Michael and Robert reached the log boats just as one was ready for boarding. Michael grabbed at some folded bin bags on a bench. He knew that Robert could take a splash or two, but a soaking would be disaster for his robot. He knelt and pulled the boat back to the dock to enable Robert to clatter into the vessel. Once Robert was seated Michael lowered a foot to get aboard himself. Robert extended a hand as if to assist. Grabbed Michael's ankle and lifted. Sending him cartwheeling backwards. Thudding down on the wooden decking.

'What on earth?' Michael spluttered. 'Why'd you do that?'

'Robert will handle this now.' Robert's words were muffled by the gurgling water and the loud ripples of his craft. It pulled into the main stream and glided away.

Michael watched Robert disappear round the first bend. A gentle drifting motion in the swirling murky water.

Victor too saw Robert vanish along the preliminary course of the ride. He knew the layout of the attraction. Knew where his quarry was heading. And knew these 'boats' ran on the same gauge rail as the roller coaster.

Michael stared incredulously as the giant robot produced wheels for each limb, saw Victor attach them to the half-submerged track and move off in pursuit of his escaping friend, Robert.

It was puzzling behaviour by Robert, but as Michael ran down the hill to the splash pool he was fearful that Victor would catch his robot and could only imagine what foul deed that grotesque monster was planning.

'Look!' A father crouching down to his two young children pointed to the gushing water above the steep descent of *Kamikaze Tsunami*. 'It's that tatty old robot. And there! There behind him. See it? The gleaming metal one. Spanking new, eh? Boy this show's good, don't you think?'

The children screwed their eyes and laughed. Clowns at the circus. 'What's he going to do now, Daddy?'

Of course Daddy didn't know. No one did. Only the children who had witnessed the great escape at *Dragon's Lair* suspected it wasn't going to be pleasant. They huddled together; eyes fixed on Robert's fragile craft perched at the lip of the falls.

Robots don't scream. Every log boat that had ever made that final plunge was brim full of shrieking passengers. Now there was only silence. Robert shot down the falling water without a murmur. Only the flash of the photograph. On impact the placid lake detonated. Spray like platinum rods impaled the air. Lashing water blitzed the surface.

And through the mist Robert slid to a crawl. Upright. Unmoved by the experience. As logical as a robot.

Above him the brutal mass of Victor toppled over the edge of the cascading water. Not constricted by the cog railway system that controlled Robert's carriage, Victor plummeted down. Barbaric acceleration. Crushing weight hurtling towards Robert's gliding boat. A sitting target.

Robert hadn't been idle on his pedestrian journey to the final descent. He had carefully hauled on to each of his paint pot legs a plastic bin bag. With surprising agility he leapt from his boat into the thigh-deep water. Risking the waterproof capacity of his arms he thrust them down to the track beneath. Plucked the rails from the sleepers and dragged them sideways. In his makeshift waders he carried the bending steel runners to deeper water.

Victor exploded onto the lake. He gave a screeching cry of battle. Zoomed along the straight. Wheels carrying him like lightning. And when he thought, and Donald viewing from his hideout thought, he was about to crush the puny pile of scrap...the track he was stuck to no longer ran straight. And Victor was taken in a vicious curve, out of his depth. Out into the deepness of the lake, where even his massive bulk would sink far enough down to...malfunction!

Sizzle! Fizzle! Phut!

'Fantastic stuff!' A middle-aged man acknowledged. Flapping his applauding hands like a seal. 'Grand show.'

Clapping erupted from the crowd.

'A magnificent spectacle.'

'Brilliantly staged.'

'Did you see the scabby one in the junk suit do that?'

'Lightning speed.'

'Incredible timing. What a display.'

An appreciative audience.

Victor fell from the rails. Tipped over and started to sink at the shoulder. Low groan. Just like a felled statue. An image out of favour. Loud crackles and blue sparks accompanied his drowning. The fishy odour of short-circuiting.

Donald lost contact. Jasper crept away.

Victor could not respond. He rolled over onto his front and floated.

Dead.

Michael ran through the water and helped Robert ashore. Hailed as a hero. A true one to those who knew the whole story, and celebrity adulation from those who had witnessed nothing more than what they thought to be a showbiz spectacular.

Blue lights flashed and sirens blasted. The fat man had called the police once he had seen Victor lumbering through the park.

'Blooming hell!' Harry Evans tore off his cap and kicked it. 'It's the bleeding robot again!'

'I don't believe it.' Sergeant Billet flopped to a halt behind his constable. 'I'm jacking this flipping job in if this carries on. Where's the blooming real criminal gone? You know, flesh and bleeding bone. I'm blooming haunted by bleeding metal, bleeding robots.'

'Take it easy Sergeant.' Michael pulled at his sleeve. 'Robert has solved the mystery for you.'

'You! Up to the same ruddy nonsense I bet.'

'Look there.' Michael pointed to the marooned torso of Victor, partially submerged, bobbing in the lake. 'That's your robber. And the one who rampaged through the school. Robert caught him for you.'

Sergeant Billet scratched his head and surveyed the scene. Sensed the warmth in the crowd for the rust-bucket robot. Saw the shape floating in the lake. 'Harry, Pete. Take some statements here. I'm getting some sort of picture, but I want a clear one. You know how hazy anything to do with damn robots can be.'

Billet was cornered by the fat man. Michael couldn't hear their conversation. The fat man was pointing to *Dragon's Lair* and then to the water chute in front of him. And pulling Billet by the elbow he indicated a large removal truck parked on the service road. Billet took hold of Robert and marched him away, notebook flapped open. He was following a scent.

After half-an-hour Billet returned dragging a reluctant boy beside him. Donald Clipper was whelping like a spoilt girl. 'Harry, leave that and wander around the undergrowth. See if you can find that weirdo that belongs to this fellow. He'll be bent over behind a bush muttering to himself and dribbling. And he'll most likely start bleating about how innocent he is if he's cornered. You know the guy. Uncle Jasper.' Billet gave a knowing smile.

'It's that git Clipper.' A tall spotty kid announced.

'Yeah.' Mystified recognition by all the school-kids.

'What's he doing here?' Michael asked. He hadn't completed the jigsaw yet.

'Now, for once, I have one over on you Michael Dobbins,' Billet began. 'This chappy here.' Billet yanked Donald by the ear and into Michael's face. 'This chappy here is the owner of that monstrosity there.' Billet nodded towards the whale-like roundness rocking in the water. 'Apparently goes by the name of Victor. A robot of dubious character and morals, devised by young Donald Clipper and built by his sinister Uncle Jasper. They were out to destroy your *charming* lump of tin, Robert. It was Donald's party. Not that you care now. Sent those invites just so he could ambush your friend. Amazing how talkative a child can be when you have him sandwiched between a police officer and a peeved robot.'

Harry stumbled out of the bushes. Uncle Jasper under his arm. No kid gloves with this villain.

'Ah, a complete set.' For once Sergeant Billet seemed pleased.

'We'll take these two away. Think we might be able to get them for attempted assault with a deadly weapon.' Billet grinned. 'So you, m'lad, watch your step with that tin pot, the law isn't going to stand for any more fun and games with flipping robots from now on.'

Donald and Jasper were hauled off in a police van, and left just before the rescue vehicle arrived to tow Victor's corpse from the water.

Robert was no lightweight, but all the children knew a hero, and how to treat one. With a countdown and a mighty effort they hoisted him onto their shoulders. It wasn't pretty but it was the thought that counted. Sprawled across several kids. Legs spread and arms whirling. And a very average rendition of *he's a jolly good fellow* accompanied the giddy entourage out of the park.

Chapter Seventeen

'You're in this one as well.' Michael struggled with the large sheets of the newspaper. 'We can see who's going to be a big head all right. Look at this photo.'

Robert sat at the kitchen table. He was allowed that honour now that he was the local hero. Not that Gran thought it was right. Then she'd moan about anything.

'Certainly a celebrity now.' Michael wrestled with a further unwieldy page of the broadsheet. 'It's going to be hard sticking you down in the basement with all this interest in your adventures.'

Robert peered at the page Michael was reading. Tilted his head to see it properly. 'Robert looks good in his picture.' A sign of vanity from the robot. 'A handsome robot don't you think, Master?' Robert's crisp steel voice echoed around the kitchen.

'To be honest, Robert, and no hard feelings, you aren't the smartest looking robot. And that's my fault.' Michael quickly added. 'I was scraping about a bit when I made you. In fact you're really a collection of bits and pieces nobody wanted. Except maybe Gran's biscuit tins.'

'What was that? You mention my biscuits? You

been up there, in my room again?' Gran pounced on Michael's words.

'No, no, Gran. Take it easy.' Michael held up his hands in surrender.

'Hmm.' Gran waddled off down the hallway, muttering. She'd check her biscuits, just in case.

'As I was saying, Robert, you are a very tatty looking robot. Sorry if that hurts your feelings, but you really are a scruffy assembly of assorted junk.'

Robert clanked to his feet and clattered off in the direction that Gran had taken.

'Robert! Only being honest. Don't want you to think you sparkle like a new pin.' Michael sensed he had been too truthful. He scampered after his robot.

Robert was standing in his corner of the basement when Michael found him. 'You all right, Robert?'

'Robert is junk.' Sadness in his tinny voice.

'Don't take it to heart. Come on let's go out. Everyone will be pleased to see the champion.'

'No, Robert will stay here. Robert doesn't want to go out now he knows he looks so unattractive.'

Michael wished he'd been more subtle. He'd put his foot in it, big time. He didn't realise you could upset a robot that easily.

At dinner that evening Robert stayed below, sulking.

'You're quiet, Michael,' his mother observed. 'With

all this excitement I would expect you to be buzzing. The whole town is full of tales about you and Robert.'

'It's Robert. I decided, like an idiot, to tell him he didn't look the hero. You know, just stuff about the odds and ends he's made of.'

'Go steady, son.' Mr. Dobbins spoke through a mouthful of pasta. 'Even a robot gets hurt when you undermine his confidence.' He cleared a stray loop of spaghetti hanging from his chin. Suddenly he was a robot expert.

'Yeah.' Michael parked his cutlery and excused himself from the table.

The arrival of Cecil Spinks from Grumleys store later in the week was more of a shock than a surprise. Michael feared the worse. What had Robert done now? Were we back in the old routine? One problem with that crazy tin can after another.

'Special delivery,' Spinks announced. Official, but with a twinkle in his eye. 'For Robert.' He placed three large boxes just inside the door, touched his forehead with something like a salute and left.

'What are these?' Michael lifted the packages and let them drop. A hollow rattle. 'Not that heavy. Noisy though.'

'Was that a consignment from Grumleys?' Michael's father enquired.

'Yes. What is it?' Michael was puzzled.

'Fine. Nothing to worry about.' Mr. Dobbins sucked in air and puffed out his chest.

'Manager delivered the boxes. That Spinks guy. Said they were for Robert.'

'And so they are. Now run along and get your mother. Then pop down to the basement and bring Robert up here. Understand?'

'Okay, Dad.' Michael wasn't okay about it at all. What was going on? It was strange activity for the Dobbins' household.

Robert plodded up the stairs from where he was hiding. He was ugly. His master had told him. He wouldn't go out. The basement was just fine.

'Ah, Robert.' Mr. Dobbins greeted the robot with a cock of the head and a broad grin.

Mrs. Dobbins was in her neat, pale blue suit and looking pleased with herself.

Michael fingered the sleeves of his sweatshirt. This wasn't a usual family gathering. Something was going on and he was far from comfortable.

Bill Dobbins coughed to clear his throat.

Michael's shoulders drooped. He was finding it all very embarrassing.

'Robert, you're a special robot and sort of part of the family.' Mr. Dobbins swallowed.

Michael cringed.

'These are for you.' Mr. Dobbins held out his arms

to show he meant all the boxes on the floor.

'Thank you.' Robert didn't know why Michael's father would present him with boxes, but he had to be polite. He picked two of them up and was about to take them to the basement.

'No, no, Robert. You must open them. It's the contents that are for you.'

'Duh!' Michael murmured.

'Robert pulled at the tape that secured the first package. It sprang apart. Robert shoved his face deep into the box, and stayed there. Sounds like the cooing of a wood-pigeon escaped from the gap between the robot's head and box flaps.

'What do you think?' Mr. Dobbins bent down and spoke into the gap.

'Yes. Very good. Beautiful.' Robert plucked his head out of the dark.

Michael convulsed with laughter. Robert had emerged with shredded paper packing fixed to his bucket head like a grey wig.

Mrs. Dobbins rushed to remove the curls from Robert's head.

'So what's in the box that's so great?' Michael enquired after he had calmed down.

Robert tipped the cardboard container over. A collection of the brightest paint pots you've ever seen. Tumbling and rolling, the gleaming tins cluttered the floor.

'Wow!' exclaimed Michael.

'Your new limbs, Robert.' Mr. Dobbins held two of the tins together to demonstrate how it would look. 'Classy, eh?'

'And the other packages?' Michael enquired.

'Open those, Robert. You'll be just as pleased.' Mr. Dobbins was getting excited.

Robert ripped open the remaining boxes. Out spilled a sparkling, galvanised bucket and a rather attractive matching dustbin. The very essence of a twenty-first century robot. Robert hugged the dustbin and examined the bucket. Occasionally placing them together. Just to see what he would eventually look like.

'Seems I've got my work cut out,' Michael joked. 'It's going to take all my spare time to put you back together as a real dude.'

'You'll have help, of course.' Michael's dad tapped his chest. 'A capable assistant.'

'Yeah.' Michael winked at his dad.

'And, Robert.' Mrs. Dobbins broke into this all-male moment. 'This is also for you.' She held out a bulging plastic bag.

Robert stood the bucket on the dustbin and took a step towards her. 'For me?' It really was a good day.

'Now, a lot of estimation involved. If they're not

right I'll get them altered.' Mrs. Dobbins was feeling awkward.

Robert delved into the bag. Retrieving from inside a bundle of material. He laid it on the floor and stepped back.

'That's amazing.' Michael looked down on a complete set of clothes. Clothes for a robot! Trousers in a dark blue. Flared ones that were all the rage. A blazing red sweater that Mrs. Dobbins had knitted conscientiously every evening for a fortnight. Sleeves to accommodate Robert's potty arms, and a high turtle-neck to hide some of the ugly welded joints. To crown it all there was the coolest bobble hat in a splendid shade of orange. Making hats for buckets is not easy, but Mrs. Dobbins had skilfully managed to produce the perfect headgear for a robot.

Trying on his entire wardrobe would wait. Robert was far too sensitive to be seen struggling into clothing he knew little about. But the bobble hat couldn't be resisted, and he tentatively perched it on his head.

'Excellent!' Michael was delighted.

'Take a look.' Mrs. Dobbins held out her hand mirror.

'Mmm.' Robert viewed his new hat from every angle. 'Mmm.' It was all he could utter. Proud as punch.

'Pleased?' Mr. Dobbins enquired.

'Thanks, Mum.' Michael gave his mum a peck on the cheek.

'Robert will be the most handsome robot ever.' Robert gripped the mirror tight and seemed to waltz around to imaginary music. Purring at his image.

Truly, Robert the robot was indeed contented.

And the casual observer, peeking into the Dobbins' front room would have seen the fixed grins of a family, arm in arm, entertained by the sweeping movements of their dancing robot. A robot whose troubles and adventures were far from over.